The Empress Trilogies

Betrothal & Betrayal
Poison Is A Woman's Weapon
Seizing Power
The Price of Eyes

By Janet McGiffin
Illustrated by Harry Pizzey

Book I

Betrothal & Betrayal

Scotland Street Press

Published in 2023 by
Scotland Street Press
Edinburgh

A CIP record for this book is available from the British Library.

ISBN: 978-1-910895-788

Typeset by Tommy Pearson
Printed on responsibly sourced paper
Cover image and design by Harry Pizzey

*Many thanks to Jean, Paddy, Harry,
Susan, Katerina, and Nellie.*

EMPIRE OF THE R

during the life of

1. IKONION   6. PENDYKION
2. FILOMELION 7. NICOMEDIA
3. AMORION   8. HIERIA
4. DORYLAION 9. PROPONTIS SEA
5. NICAEA

AVARS

SLAVS

PAPAL
STATE

ROME

THESSALONIKI

CALABRIA

SICILY

ATHENS

AEGE

CRETE

ROMAN

NS OF THE EAST

aens • Circa 770 ad

AVS

KHAZARS

GOTHS

KHERSON

PONTUS SEA

CONSTANTINOPLE

9   8 7

6

5

ARMENIAC THEME

ANKYRA

4

NO
MANS
LAND

3   2

1

BAGHDAD

ANTIOCH

CALIPHATE

CYPRUS

0   100   200

CONSTANTINOPLE
Circa 770 ad.

1. FORUM OF CONSTANTINE
2. HIPPODROME
3. BASILICA CISTERN
4. MILION
5. DAPHNE PALACE
6. AUGUSTAION
7. CHURCH OF HOLY WISDOM
8. SENATE
9. CHALKE GATE
10. CHURCH OF ST IRINI

MESI STR

LYCUS RIV.

CEMETERY
OF PELAGIOS

0   ½   One Roman Mile

PUBLIC BATHS

MESI STREET

TA GASTRIA
CONVENT

STUDIOS MONASTERY

GOLDEN GATE

PRISON

N

Chapter I

Our pig got away from me when I was easing him into the pen and Father wouldn't leave him run free in the pasture since we would be gone all day, so I had to chase him down and it was my fault that we were late getting to Ikonion with Father cursing me the whole way.

"May I be damned once and damned twice if this isn't the last day we waste trying to get you married. If Myrizikos doesn't show up again, you'll wed the grave-digger or go to the convent. You hear me, Thekla?"

The whole village heard him, may they choke on their laughing tongues.

The May sun was high in the sky when we got to the city gates—me in my mother's wedding tunica, her and my father and Myrizikos's family in their best, and old Father Damianos trundling along on his spindly legs. The ramp was jammed with families scanning the plain for their sons and brothers, praying they had survived the latest campaign against the armies of the Caliph, praying they still had their fingers and hands and some decent plunder. Soldiers were coming up the ramp and calling to the whores waiting at the gates in all the Greek accents of the Empire of the Romans of the East. Two soldiers in quilted jerkins with their bows and quivers strapped across their backs turned their dusty faces towards me.

"Hey, pretty koukla, little doll, weren't you here last year?" one called.

The other pointed at his crotch. "I'll make you a real woman."

"May your bread turn to poison in your mouth!" I hissed.

Laughter came from around me. Was there a soul in Ikonion who didn't know I had been stood up twice?

"Thekla, stupid girl, you wrote to Myri, didn't you?" my father shouted. "You wrote we would be waiting for him with Father Damianos to get you wed? Father Damianos won't give my money back this time, may God punish his greed," he added with a dark look at the priest who ignored him.

"The postal courier put my letter in his pouch, Father," I muttered, hiding my face under my wind-blown hair. I whispered to my tiny icon of Saint Thekla knotted in the corner of my scarf loosely wrapped around my throat. "Bring Myri home this year, don't let my brothers bring back another excuse."

Columns of imperial infantry were still marching in far across the plain, pipers setting the pace for the ragged tramp of boots. Every year, it fair took my breath away, our boys six abreast across the arrow-straight stone road that our Roman ancestors had laid across the plains of Anatolia. Warhorses screamed in whistling bursts, swords and helmets flashed in the sun, slaves were raising tent poles to the tune of soldiers' curses. And wasn't that Emperor Constantine himself? I strained my eyes. Yes, there he was on his white warhorse, bringing our armies home himself from the eastern frontier. I drew a breath at the sight of the powerful warrior who had ruled us since long before I was born.

"Constantine the Shitter," my father muttered, using the Emperor's nickname for what he had done in his baptismal font. He glared at our emperor chatting with his sons and his commanders while his tent city rose up around him. Emperor Constantine, Hand of God on Earth, Christ's Vice-Regent, Defender and Champion of the Faith, the fifth Constantine after the Great one who built Constantinople. He was a giant of a man with fair hair tied back with a strap, a broad moustache and fair beard trimmed so short that it was hardly there. That spring he was forty-five years old and had worn the jewelled crown of Emperor of the Roman Empire of the East for most of his life.

He swung himself off his mount, copied by his three sons. The oldest, Co-emperor Leon, was eighteen and would be our next emperor when his father died even though he had yet to command a unit. His half-brothers Christoforos and Nikiforos were fourteen and eleven. The Emperor had just named them as kaisars. A younger son was in the Great Palace in Constantinople, a daughter, too.

"Three wives and four sons!" breathed Myrizikos's father with the aching envy of a man with one son and the rest daughters. "First wife gives him Leon the Useless and dies. Second wife dies and the baby too. But does our emperor give up lifting his sword? No! He got himself a real breeder." He elbowed my father in the gut—two peas in a pod, they were, short, thick, and greying, with quick eyes and quicker tempers.

The army commanders were climbing off their mounts. We knew them; they camped on the plains every campaign: Mihalis the Dragon was the Emperor's favourite, he always led the campaigns. Then there was Mihalis Melissinos who had married the empress's sister, and Mamikonian who led the famed army of the Anatolia theme. Beside him was Tatzates who led the army of the theme of Boukellaria. The emperor's tent was up now, red banner flapping. Next they would set up his massive linen bathtub and fill it with our river water.

"He burns our wood to heat his bath," my father muttered, like every year. "He conscripts our sons. His armies strip the bread from our bakeries, foul our river, and eat down our pasture. They burn our charcoal and timber, their wagons break our roads and bridges. On top of that, he taxes the goat milk I sell, the tools I buy, the land I till. He would tax the stars above if he could."

We knew they would be back today. Our neighbours had met the scouts out inspecting the plain and river banks where the army would camp. Even this far inside the empire, bands of raiders from the Caliphate could ambush a tired column of returning infantry.

"No men captured or lost in battle," the neighbour had reported. "Booty and prisoners for slaves. The main column is camped ten miles south. A day's march."

When my brothers and Myrizikos had turned fourteen, they had registered their names on the record of their obligation to serve. Once a year, they had to report to the muster point with their weapons. Commanders chose their conscripts by age, fitness, and weapons. Slaves didn't serve. Neither did men born into hereditary service, like town counsellors. Or heretics, priests, convicted adulterers, and those dishonourably discharged. My brothers were infantry archers in the Anatolia theme army. They made their own bows and arrows and my mother sewed their quilted jerkins. Only imperial soldiers got uniforms and weapons. Myrizikos was a mounted archer because his father could afford a mule. Two years ago, the three of them had been called up to fight at the border, right after our betrothal ceremony. It was a month before the wedding. Myrizikos was sixteen; I was fifteen. The first year, he didn't come back with my brothers. He had been transferred into an imperial unit that needed skilled archers, they said. The second year they said he had been promoted and couldn't be spared. A boy becomes a man during those years. What does a girl become? Too old to find a husband, that's what.

I sat down and put my back to the city wall. Now my mother's wedding tunica was too short. My legs in my undyed wool knotted stockings stuck out like a chicken. I spat. The water from my leather flask hadn't cleared the vomit in my mouth. I had lost my breakfast porridge on the way here. Nerves.

My mother and my oldest brother's hugely pregnant wife were sprawled in the shade with Myri's mother and four sisters. "Bind your hair; you're not a child!" shouted my mother. I ignored her. Few women bound their hair anymore. I refused to cover my mouth and nose with my scarf either. Only old women did that.

Father Damianos was dozing in the sun. Three generations of our village had grown up hearing his prayers for each life-passage. He read them from his prayer codex: prayers after a child's first steps, prayers before the first haircut, prayers before the first shave. He blessed our cottages and our sheep and goats. We learned to read by struggling through his codex, the Rule of Saint Basil. He said that Saint Basil believed that prayer was part of life. This made sense to me since I was always praying not to be beaten for something I did or didn't do. Father Damianos also had the small codex of the Ekloga, the laws that governed us. When Myrizikos didn't come back that first year, Father Damianos had called both our families to his cottage and sternly explained the marriage laws.

"If two years pass after a betrothal and there is no marriage, Thekla can call Myrizikos before witnesses and demand that he marry her or say in public that he won't. If he won't, the betrothal gift is hers to keep and she can marry another. If Myrizikos can't be found after two years, Thekla keeps the gift and can marry another."

If I could find a man to marry. Plenty of miserable spinsters lived out their lives in their brothers' houses or the convent of Agia Piste, the Holy Faith, inside the walls of Ikonion. It was a dingy hole ruled by a sharp-tongued abbess who half-starved the nuns on a diet of Saint's Broth, also called Shit Soup—water, onions, herbs, and a few drops of oil poured over dry bread. The abbess and her assistant nuns dined on richer fare, may God punish their gluttony.

Myrizikos's father had given the priest a limp smile. "Myri is a soldier, Father. He has to go where he is sent."

"A betrothal is a vow taken with the name of God," Father Damianos had thundered. "If Myrizikos breaks his vow, he is denying God. This is punished by excommunication under canon law and exile or mutilation under civil law."

Two years I had waited at the gates. This was the third. I watched the travellers coming out of the city gates and going down the steep ramp to the caravans of coaches lined up outside the walls. There were wagon caravans too being loaded with rugs, glass vessels and leather goods to be sold in Amorion and the other big towns along the road to Constantinople. Ikonion women were famed rug makers. Not me. I couldn't cook, knot stockings, stitch clothes, or weave rugs. The knife and sling were my tools and I carried them on my belt. Everyone carried a knife to eat with, but I also used mine to slit the throats of rabbits and chickens and warn off my uncles when their hands got too near. One stone in my sling could bring down an eagle or hawk hovering above my new-born lambs and kids.

An old granny smiled sweetly at me as she and a younger woman moved down the slippery cobblestones. "May you be blessed with a rich husband and children, my child."

"And a humble tongue." This came from a tall muscular monk behind her carrying two heavy carpetbags and a satchel. His shabby tunica and sandals looked like monk's garb, and he was clean-shaven like a monk. But I saw no bald spot in his thick dark hair where his tonsure should have been.

"May you drown in your wine, krasopatera, wino monk!" I snarled. My mother laughed even as she crossed herself. Most monks in Ikonion were degenerate drunkards who hung about the markets swiping food. They were ex-soldiers who had no pension and had taken the vows to put a roof over their heads. They wandered the roads as the spirit moved them. Patriarch Nikitas in Constantinople had issued a ban on itinerant monks. Monks were supposed to join a monastery and stay there.

A furtive movement caught my eye. My father had his head together with our village grave-digger who was also our bone-scraper. He was a skeletal man with four teeth. He buried our dead and then dug them up after seven years, scraped the bones clean, and put them in wooden ossuaries, stone if the family was rich. The ossuaries were stacked in the crypt of our village church. He lived in a hut by the cemetery with his two dim-witted sons. His wife had died, taken by the ghosts of poorly-scraped bones, people whispered.

Horror sucked out my breath. I scuttled over to my mother. She was reminding everyone who would listen how she had twice embroidered flowers onto her wedding dress to make it look new for me.

"I'm not marrying the bone-scraper. I will die first," I hissed.

My mother grabbed my arm so hard it hurt. "I am not going to another wedding and hearing, 'May Thekla be next.' If Myri doesn't come, you will marry the bone-scraper. We need your bed for your brother's children, bless them."

My sister-in-law smirked. My hand itched to slap her. I clutched my icon of Saint Thekla of Ikonion First Woman Martyr and Equal to the Apostles. She was born in Ikonion and was the patron saint. Father Damianos had slipped the tiny bit of wood between my infant hands when he had baptised me with her name. His faith gave him courage. Long before I was born, our emperor had banned icons. When he died, his son, our Emperor Constantine, had proclaimed that anyone having an icon would have their ear or nose cut off. He had ordered soldiers to burn monasteries where monks and nuns were painting icons. I kept Saint Thekla well hidden. Besides, we were far from Constantinople and any icon-burning soldiers.

The bone-scraper slunk off with a sly smile on his purple lips. My father went on ranting. When I was born, my family had been living near the border with the Caliphate. A peddler had come through warning that Emperor Constantine's soldiers were setting fire to villages and fields to make a 'No Man's Land'. That way, Caliph al-Mansur's raiders could not so easily steal our livestock and drag us off as slaves. We were all to be transferred to the border of the Bulgar Khanate.

"He burnt our fields and houses," muttered my father. "He drove us from land that was ours since the Great Alexander. We—who paid our taxes as loyal citizens and sent our sons as soldiers—we were to be herded away like sheep. But we escaped his treachery and walked here to Anatolia."

My father would have gone on for hours if Myri's father had not cut him off with a joyful shout. "Our boys are home!"

And there they came in their leather caps, bows and quivers across their backs, slings swinging on their belts. My oldest brother was leading a heavily-laden mule.

"That's my mule!" exclaimed Myri's father, looking frightened. "Where's my boy? Where's Myrizikos?"

"Dead! Killed!" Myri's mother wailed.

I went cold. Would I be a widow before I was even married?

"Myri's alive and well!" my older brother shouted, hearing the wails as he yanked the mule up the ramp. "Emperor Constantine spotted Myri's skill and chose him for his personal guard, the Tagmata. Here's your mule, sir. Myri is riding a horse from the imperial stables at Malagina."

Even my mother's non-stop mouth went quiet. Our eyes turned towards the Emperor's tent where the imperial flag waved in the spring breeze.

Relief flooded me. "Myrizikos is over there! We will marry!"

"No, Thekla," my brother said. "Myri is on a warship. He's guarding some Monophysite refugees. They came across in a prisoner exchange. We gave the Caliph back his soldiers we had captured; they gave us some Monophysite heretics they had captured. Emperor Constantine has ordered them sent to the Bulgar border. They can't cause trouble there. Myri is escorting them."

We crossed ourselves. Monophysites believed that Jesus Christ had only one nature and that was divine.

The truth, Father Damianos said, was that Jesus had two natures, divine and human. Monophysites caused fights wherever they went.

I glimpsed the pocked face of the bone-scraper lurking in the crowd. I grabbed my brother's arm desperately. "How can Myri be in the Emperor's guard if the Emperor is here and Myri's on a warship?"

My brother lost what little patience he had. He raised his voice. "The Emperor is inspecting the town fortifications, Thekla. Teaching his three sons, if those fools can learn anything. Then he'll go south to the port of Syke and get on a warship. He'll inspect the forts at Piraeas and along the Aegean Sea. Myri will join him at Thessaloniki. It's a real honour to be in the Tagmata. Myri could be named patrikios and even sit at the Emperor's table at banquets!"

He untied a leather purse from the cord around his neck and handed it to Myrizikos's mother. "Myri's army pay." He pointed at the bundles roped to the saddle on the mule. "His booty from the campaign. He did well."

Myrizikos's mother spilled the coins out on her palm. "An imperial salary," she whispered with awe. "A horse from the Malagina stables."

Awkwardly, his father turned to me. "Thekla, my girl, Myri always dreamed of being an imperial soldier. The first year he didn't come home, I told your father to end the betrothal and let him go free. But your mama said no. And the next year, no."

I turned on my mother, shaking with fury and shame. "Why? I could have married another."

"Who? You can't cook or sew. You have a nasty temper.

And you're old. No man wants a dried currant when he can have a plump grape."

The bone-scraper was edging nearer.

My father glanced at him. "You'll wed the grave-digger, girl. I paid Father Damianos for a wedding today and by God we're going to have one."

"Myri will come back here when he gets leave," I said, desperately. "We'll wed then."

"Thekla, open your ears!" my younger brother shouted. "Myri is a guard for the Emperor. He will live in the barracks in Constantinople. He will have his own seal. He will be paid in gold coins. He will not marry you."

I could hear the desperation in my voice. "Myri will be waiting for me in Constantinople. I will go there and we will wed. Or he will say that he won't. That's the law, isn't it, Father Damianos." I believed it, too. Every word I said that day, I believed. It wasn't just hope.

My mother's slap caught me full across the face. "This is your fault, girl. What did you do to drive Myri away?"

"She didn't do it the way he likes it," smirked my younger brother.

"Because he liked how you do it better!" I shouted, holding my hand to my smarting cheek. Who hadn't seen Myrizikos and the other boys laughing and splashing their naked bodies in the river, their slippery limbs twisting around each other.

My brother's fist shot out. I ducked. I ran down the ramp towards the plateia, looking for somewhere to hide. Three coaches were moving out, whips cracking, mules lunging into their harnesses. The fourth coach was being held up by the old woman I had seen coming down the ramp. She was refusing to get inside, shrieking and struggling like a terrified sheep. The younger woman was trying to drag her. The mules were rearing in fright, the mounted guards were shouting, and the coachman was bellowing he was leaving them behind.

Old people who are afraid, their ears don't hear. I slipped my arm around the old granny and leaned against her, ducking down to hide. My body calmed her, like when I calm a frightened sheep. A few steps forward and we were inside the coach with the younger woman right behind. The door slammed, the coach jerked forward, and I ducked down. Too late! My brother had spotted me and was chasing us even as we picked up speed.

The younger woman didn't see him. She clutched my hands. "The angels have sent you, koritzaki. My mother's wits are gone. I can't handle her. She trusts you. Help me take her to my brother in Amorion. I'll pay you a silver milaresion and send you home by coach."

All around me became still and quiet, sharp and clear as a spring morning. I felt the pressure of her hands on mine, I saw the monk who had been behind them sitting opposite me with two other men. I heard the clatter of mules' hooves on cobblestones. I heard my voice, easy and confident.

"Two milaresia and never mind the coach back."

At that moment, my brother jumped onto the running board and stuck his angry face into the window. He fumbled at the door handle. "Get out of this coach, Thekla malakismeni!" he shouted.

The monk stretched out a hand and held the handle closed. He spoke gently to the woman, now shrinking

23

back in terror.

"Ignore the lad, Despina. My cousin has squabbled with her brother since they were infants. She is a humble girl—a perfect companion for your dear mother."

The woman promptly dug into her coin purse and held up two milaresia. But my brother's quick fist shot through the window and snatched them. My knife flew into my hand. I grabbed the cord around my brother's neck that held his wooden cross and his coin purse. I slit it, yanking the purse inside and elbowing his face sharply as I did. His bellow of pain and fury as he tumbled backwards brought a shout of laughter from the men.

I smiled sweetly at them and spilled the contents of the purse onto my palm. It was his army pay: shining silver milaresia and copper folles. I selected two milaresia.

Then, as I am an honest person, I replaced the rest and flipped the purse out the window for him to retrieve from the dust.

Chapter II

Our Roman ancestors left us with a system of roads and roadbeds that are teeth-rattling torture—round stones the size of my fist, or larger round stones with smaller stones in between, or oblong stones with thinner flat stones between. Inside Ikonion, the gaps were filled with cement. Not so on the open road.

I braced myself to keep from being rattled off the wooden bench. Panic struck. I was on a coach with five people I didn't know, travelling to a place I had never been, with all I owned being my mother's wedding tunica, my knife, sling, and three silver milaresia, two of which I hadn't earned yet. How could I have imagined I could go to Constantinople! I would return home from Amorion on the first coach, I told myself to calm the panic. I was wrong, as I learned the hard way. When you step on a path, you go where it goes and there's nothing to do but keep walking.

My decision eased my panic, however, and I ran my eyes over my travelling companions. The monk, if he indeed was a monk, had well-muscled shoulders under his shabby tunic and an easy smile which I ignored. The other two men were wine merchants, they told us politely. After that, we spoke little, the jolting and creaking coach making conversation impossible. At mid-day, we stopped outside a small army fort by a clear stream. The soldiers in the watch tower opened the gates and our guards went inside to talk to the commander. We sat in the soft spring grass to eat.

My employer pulled out slices of cured ham, raisins, and double-baked paximadia rusks. I took them to the stream to soften and the old lady nibbled on one. But she looked pale and shaky and could eat no more. I quickly ate her meal as my stomach was burning with hunger. Then I took the old lady behind some bushes to relieve herself, followed by a stroll to ease her stiff joints. We ate some blackberries which stained her tunica and she started weeping that her daughter would shout at her, poor witless thing.

The monk, Brother Elias, as he claimed his name was, heard her sobs and came over with words of comfort. He had a deep mellow voice, which I had noticed when he was telling my employer to hire me. The poor old granny fastened her helpless eyes on him and stopped her tears. He spoke politely to me. As he didn't stink of sweat and sour wine like the fake or footloose monks who wandered the roads and lounged in the Ikonion markets, I took my hand off my knife and let him chat.

"Emperor Constantine had these small forts built where robbers or raiders from the Caliph's army might attack," he explained. "If there is danger, the commander will have soldiers escort us to the next fort. The commander knows the danger situation because, at set times, every fort sends a courier to the next fort stating their situation. Anything serious and they get a message to a beacon tower and flame signals can reach the Emperor in Constantinople in a day."

My brothers had told me about these signal towers that marched from mountain top to mountain top from Constantinople to the far corners of the empire, one within flame sight of the next. I climbed back into the coach, feeling safer that our Emperor knew where we were. The old lady fell asleep as did I. When I awoke, we were at Tyraion, a market town and army garrison, said Brother Elias, a real fountain of information. We rattled through the iron-studded wooden gates behind the other three coaches and pulled up in a wide plateia shaded by mulberry trees. I helped the old granny out and looked around.

The stench of rotting vegetables and pig swill made me feel right at home. Soldiers shouted sweet-talk at me. I pulled my scarf over my nose and mouth to hide my smile, enjoying their silly praises without my mother there to shout curses at them and drag me away. Brother Elias handed me two carpet bags that he said belonged to my employer. She and her mother had joined the women from the other carriages and were walking down a narrow lane.

"What about their trunk?" I asked Brother Elias.

"Trunks stay on the coach locked inside the stable. Drivers and guards sleep in the loft. You're sleeping in the convent."

I hurried after my employer, throwing a quick look over my shoulder. The monk was going into a nice-looking inn. Not a real monk, then. Monks stayed in monasteries. Resigned to a wooden plank for a bed and Saint's Broth for supper, I stepped through a heavy wooden gate. A novice, wearing a short maforion over her hair, closed it and dropped the bar into the slots.

To my pleasant surprise, around me was a flower-filled garden bounded by two-storey stone buildings, their lower walkways shaded by heavy vines. A smiling abbess wearing an undyed linen tunica to her shoes and a maforion that wrapped her hair, forehead, and chin welcomed us with clasped hands and a dip of her head. She motioned us to relax on some cushions spread under a broad plane tree. A novice passed around mugs of cool lemon water.

"When you are rested, have a wash," she said in a gentle voice. "Supper is in the refectory after Esperinos prayers."

A breeze brought the odour of boiling onions. Saint's Broth, I sighed. Still, refreshed and cheered by the cool lemon water, I got the old granny on her feet and a novice showed us to our cell.

A lovely breeze cooled our simple whitewashed chamber. I poked one of the two mattresses. Wool stuffed, with linen sheets and a wool blanket. Real luxury! The novice took us down the passage to the toilets and bathhouse. To my amazement, the toilet was not a rank hole in the ground like the communal toilet in my village, but a long wooden bench mounted over a stone trough and pierced with holes for sitting. The novice showed me how to throw a bucket of water down the trough when we were through. It disappeared under the wall.

I got the old woman toileted and sat her on a bench in the bathhouse. I stripped off her tunica and under-tunica and doused her with cool water from a stone tank. She sat peacefully while I talked soothing nonsense like I talk to our sheep. It comforted me as well, the echo of my voice against the cool walls and floor, the slosh of water against stone. I dressed her and let her sit while I washed myself. I had no change of clothes so I got back into my wedding dress, soiled and smelly as it was. I would wash it before bed in the basin in our room. I didn't put on stockings. There were no men.

In the refectory, eleven of us stood bare-footed on a soft wool rug next to cushions set around a low table, while the abbess prayed. Five women were from our caravan, I counted, wondering about the rest. We said 'Amen' and everyone got settled on cushions while the novices brought our supper. Except for me. I remained standing. In our house, my mother and I put food on the table for my father and brothers and stood while they ate so we could fill up their plates. She and I ate our supper while we cooked. My employer wiggled her fingers at me.

"Sit, kouritzaki. There are no men here who need us to serve them."

I forced my knees to bend. My hand could hardly take up the wooden spoon the novice handed me, or the wooden bowl of stew. But once my tongue tasted the delicious broad beans in a sweet and salty broth of peas and mint, I spooned it up like I was starving. The raised barley bread was fresh and chewy and sprinkled with seeds.

"Aniseed and sesame seed," my employer said when I asked. New to me! I had no idea bread could taste this good.

I was surprised to learn that the other women were not nuns. They were widows or spinsters who paid the abbess for a peaceful life. They told us without shame or guilt that they preferred this life to keeping house for their sons or brothers or uncles. They spoke happily of their garden, the scrolls and codices they were reading in the convent library, the cookery and health manuals they were writing in the scriptorium. So captivated I was by their stories that when the novices brought in the lovely smooth goat cheese with quince and persimmons steeped in honey, I looked down at my bowl and saw it was empty.

That night I got the old lady into her nightgown and into bed. Then I scrubbed out my mother's wedding tunica and hung it over the chair to dry. I set my tiny icon of Saint Thekla in the empty icon niche at the head of my bed.

"Look what money can buy!" I told her. "A cool bath, a lovely supper, and a pillow for my head! You're safe here. The abbess won't check on sleeping guests."

My bed was soft, the linen sheet smelled sweetly of rosemary as did the embroidered coverlet. My stomach smiled from the tasty meal cooked by another woman's hands. Now I knew why the rich were so cheerful.

Poor old granny, on the other hand, was ruled by

terror. The instant I blew out the candle, she shrieked for help. Frightened and confused, she climbed out of bed. She called for people her daughter later told me were long dead. Finally I gripped her in my arms and eased her into my bed. The shelter of my embrace soothed her and she dropped into an exhausted sleep.

I slept well, myself. Who wouldn't, on such a mattress! In the morning, I rose without her stirring. For a startled moment, I thought she had died. But she opened her eyes and her gaze followed me while I splashed water on my face and pulled on my mother's wedding dress. She asked my name and where we were, and allowed me to dress her. In the refectory, she devoured every bite of the semolina porridge and stewed apples spiced with something that tickled my nose and tingled my tongue. Kinammomon from the East, my employer told me. The granny drank off her infusion of sage and walked easily through the market when we bought our mid-day meal of barley rusks and cured ham and dried apricots. But a short time in the jolting carriage drained her fleeting strength and with it her wits. When we stopped at a small fort to eat, she recognized only me and from then on she clung to my hand like a child.

We stayed that night in the large fortified town of Filomelion. The convent was comfortable but did not serve supper. The nuns were fasting, it being the feast day for their saint. The abbess recommended the nearby kapelarion where she said they served cooked food and watered wine at tables. My employer was fearful to go there—she was, in general, a weak person—and she said we would fast with the nuns. To my relief, the old granny set up a howl so we crossed the lane to the kapelarion.

The place was crowded and noisy and the old lady balked at the door. I didn't know what to do, having never eaten anywhere but home, but Brother Elias spotted us and guided us to his low corner table that he was sharing with the wine merchants. We lowered ourselves onto soft cushions and he shouted at the kapelarios to bring us platters of roast venison, that being the meal of the day. Quicker than you know, a kapelarios was slamming down platters of venison grilled over charcoal, with hazelnuts, broad beans and peas, carrots, and something Brother Elias said was artichokes.

He splashed wine into our tin cups and began entertaining the old granny, easing her terror at the shouting and banging dishes and smoke billowing in from the outdoor grill. I pulled out my knife and cut her meat into small bites and she dug in like the world was just her and her wooden spoon. I stabbed my chunk of venison and took a bite. It was absolutely the best venison I had ever eaten, tender and bursting with flavour that contrasted nicely with the vegetables that were somehow both sweet and salty. An odd feeling came over me that I had never felt before. I was content! I listened to Brother Elias enchanting the old lady with his stories of Constantinople where he was born, he claimed.

"Constantine the Great saw a cross in the sky and there he built the first Christian city. Now the golden walls of Constantinople are so high that the soldiers patrolling the top are as small as sparrows. No enemy has ever breached them—even the navy of the Caliph when they attacked the sea walls with a fleet that covered the Bosporus. Emperor Leon stood on those walls and prayed while our own Emperor Constantine was being born down below in the room that was entirely purple. A great storm came up and wind blew the enemy ships off the walls. It was a sign from Heaven that God favours our empire."

My employer and her mother were still smiling when we went back to the convent. The old lady fell asleep promptly and I went to sit on a bench outside the convent gate to enjoy the silence of the evening. The air was softly scented with pines. Brother Elias came out of the inn and sat down beside me. I put my hand on my knife hilt.

"You must hide your icon better," he said in a low and urgent voice. "If the abbess spots it, she will report you to the garrison commander. He will have your tongue slit. Commander Mihalis the Dragon burnt down Pelekitis Monastery because the monks were painting icons. Emperor Constantine had the monk Andreas scourged to death in the Hippodrome because he preached the sanctity of icons. Do not think you can escape notice."

"No one saw it but you," I said defensively, but I tucked my scarf with Saint Thekla tied in the corner deeper into the neck of my tunica.

"Do you even know why they are banned?" he demanded.

"Of course. Because they are, well, banned. In the Bible. Father Damianos said."

He leaned towards me. I put my hand on my knife. He leaned away. "Icons are not banned in the Bible. Quite the reverse. I will explain so you don't lose your nose without knowing why. Emperor Leon, father of our emperor, was losing wars against the Bulgars and the Caliph. There were earthquakes. Droughts. Floods. Plague. The Emperor thought God was angry at him for allowing Jews in the empire. He ordered mass conversions. Jews all over the empire were forcibly baptised. Then the volcano on the island of Thera erupted."

"What's a volcano?"

"A volcano is a mountain that suddenly shoots fire into the sky. Smoke covers the sun for months."

"Do you practice telling lies or does it come naturally?"

He sighed. "Just accept that crops failed because smoke hid the sun. Emperor Leon next decided that God was angry because Christians were treating icons as idols and worshiping them, forbidden in the Ten Commandments. So he banned all paintings of saints or of the divine form. He tore down the icon of Christ mounted over Chalke Gate, causing riots in Constantinople.

"After he died, his son, our Emperor Constantine, didn't go after icons right away. He was fighting a civil war against his brother-in-law. He won. Then he had the invasions of the Caliph to worry about. But when his first son was born, the plague came to Constantinople and spread across the empire. Entire villages perished. Emperor Constantine's young wife died. Then his second wife, Maria, died in childbirth. So Emperor Constantine decided that God was punishing him for not enforcing his father's ban on icons. He summoned three hundred and thirty-eight bishops to Hieria Palace and locked them in for six months until they voted, in the name of the Holy Trinity—and I give you their words—'there shall be rejected and removed every likeness which is made out of any material and colour whatever by the evil art of painters.'"

"So icons are banned, like I said. I'm going to bed." I stood up.

He sighed. "I saw you in Ikonion with the priest. Let me guess. The man you were to marry didn't show up and your father was putting you in a convent."

"Not your business." I turned my back.

"Are you searching for him? Maybe I can help."

I hesitated. Brother Elias might be faking being a monk but he had helped me shake off my brother and get paid work caring for the old granny. More importantly, he knew Constantinople and I needed help finding Myrizikos. I sat down.

"Myrizikos was promoted to the Emperor's personal guard, the Tagmata. I am going to Constantinople to marry him."

"Do you know where he is posted?"

"The Tagmata."

He sighed and shook his head. "Army barracks are all over the city. Your Myrizikos could be stationed at Evdomen, seven miles away. Take my advice, go home."

"No."

"Listen to me." Elias put his hand on my arm. My knife flashed in the fading sun. He removed his hand. "Constantinople has one hundred thousand citizens plus slaves and travellers. Pickpockets will steal your purse. Merchants will cheat you. You will be assaulted and end up a whore. Find another lad."

"My father has promised me to the bone-scraper. I'm not going back." The novices were closing the gates. I went inside.

Repairs to our axle delayed our departure the next morning. My employer was in a cheerful mood, having slept two nights without her mother disturbing her. The nuns served us a delicious fresh white cheese, stewed plums, and a creamy millet porridge sweetened with honey and lavender, washed down with hot mountain tea. We went with the other women travellers to the market to buy our mid-day meal. There, we ran into Elias, also getting his meal. He had put on a clean un-dyed tunica and boots. He looked even less like a monk.

"Brother Elias," my employer said. "We have been told that there is a monk here who is a soothsayer of some repute. We want our future foretold. Can you find this monk?"

"Soothsaying is forbidden in scripture, as all good Christians should know," Elias said, crossing himself virtuously.

"Oh, what can it hurt?" smiled another woman, preventing my employer from backing down, which she would have done, given her weak nature.

"I have heard of him," he admitted, reluctantly. "He is a complete charlatan. His pronouncements are pure invention. He will take your money and say what you want to hear."

But the women insisted and, oddly enough, Elias knew exactly where to find this charlatan. He was sitting on a pile of dirty hay inside a shed propped against the wall of a monastery, obviously waiting for clients. He eagerly beckoned us inside. My employer went in with her mother while I waited with Brother Elias and the other women.

"Are you truly a monk?" I demanded to Elias in a low voice.

"Would you believe me if I said I was?"

"No."

"Then why ask?"

My employer came out, frowning. "He said I will lead a wealthy life. Of course I will. I'm a rich woman, any fool can see that." She glanced uneasily at her mother and murmured under her breath. "He also said my mother would die within two days." She crossed herself.

The old granny looked perfectly healthy to me. But I too crossed myself. I took the old lady's scrawny arm to move towards the coach but my employer stopped me.

"Your turn, Thekla. I've paid for you." She lowered her voice. "I want to know that you will be with us if my mother dies. I couldn't manage without you."

I didn't protest. A street soothsayer at the Ikonion pig market had told me that I would die a spinster alone far from home. Already I was a spinster far from home. I wanted to know about the death part. Brother Elias followed me into the shed.

The monk was still a boy, really. He took one look at Elias and jumped to his feet. "Time for prayers." He went for the door.

Brother Elias blocked him. "You have a client. Predict her future."

The monk lowered himself to the straw, keeping a cautious eye on Elias. "Hold out your palms," he told me. He stared at them intently, then folded his hands and closed his eyes. After some moments, he opened them with a frown.

"You will have a difficult and complicated life, that is clear. But there is something about rising as high as an empress. No, higher." He shook his head, puzzled.

The following night we stayed in a small walled town and garrison in the mountains. It was cold and raining. The novice who answered the bell at the convent gate said they served no food. "It's warmer in the pandohion and the food is good," she muttered, with an envious nod at the busy inn across the lane where the other travellers in our caravan were jamming through the door into a large room with tables already full of diners and a blazing fireplace and charcoal braziers pumping out heat. My employer grudgingly agreed to pay for a three-bed room. We climbed the stairs to a bedchamber that was toasty warm, being over the kapelarion. Downstairs, I devoured tender juicy roast pheasant cooked in wine with parsnips and leeks.

The old lady ate well and dozed off so my employer made me take her up to bed. I was loathe to leave the fire and the cheery wine merchants. They had invited the kapelarios to taste their wares and they were pouring liberally from their wineskins. I could hear my employer giggling and Brother Elias's laughter as I reluctantly helped the old granny up the steps.

We were both asleep when my employer rattled the door latch. She was reeking of wine. I got her boots off but she was snoring on her pillow before I could get her tunica off, so I covered her up and let her sleep in her clothes. Awake now, I held Saint Thekla between my hands and spoke to her in the dark as I had done every night for as long as I could remember. "Dear Saint Thekla, I am far from home with nothing but my cloak, my mother's wedding tunica, my knife and sling, and three silver milaresia. Why am I so happy?"

The day before we were due in Amorion, our coach broke an axle. We were passing a small fort and the commander came out to survey the damage. He was a good-looking man who spoke in an accent like the slaves in the Ikonion street market who had been captured in the Caliphate. Our scheduled stop was not far, the commander told us, and he ordered the other coaches to go on. His soldiers would accompany us to meet them tomorrow after the axle was repaired, he said. Cold rain was soaking my cloak as the soldiers dragged the coach inside the walls.

"There's no inn here," the commander told us. "You men can bed down in the barracks. For you ladies, there is a convent of sorts. The abbess takes in destitute widows and prostitutes. Pay her one copper follis for the three of you. Leave your bags inside the coach, it will be locked in the stables. Take just what you're wearing."

He directed us to a stone building near the fort entrance. The old lady whimpered as I banged on the battered door with a stone. A spy hole snapped open. I spoke into the dark hole.

"We need two rooms, with supper now and proyevma for three."

The door creaked open. The beady eyes of a bent-over crone glared at us out of a thick maforion wrapping her head and neck. Her heavy wool tunica reeked of sweat. The two nuns beside her wore equally thick tunicas and maforia that wrapped their heads warmly. Behind them, I could make out four women kneeling by a large stone mortar.

"Three silver milaresia for one cell, no food. We serve God here, not lazy guests," the crone croaked.

"One copper follis for the three of us or we sleep in the barracks," I snapped.

She held out a claw of a hand. I blocked her view of my employer's purse while she drew out the coins. We passed into the courtyard. The four women wore thin and ragged tunicas. Their maforia were of sackcloth so rough that I could see their shaven scalps. Near them, a hawk was tethered to a stake. He had pinned down a struggling rabbit with his talons. He dug his beak into the animal's body. Blood dripped on the stones.

"What a miserable place to serve God," I muttered to my employer.

"I provide a place of penance for women to redeem their sins so they can enter the Kingdom of Heaven," rasped the abbess, her ears as sharp as the hawk's beak.

She and her henchmen led us to the latrine, a stinking hole with crumbling sides. I grasped the old lady tightly while she did her business. That horror over, we followed the crone across another dank courtyard. I heard an odd chattering sound and I stopped to let my eyes adjust to the evening gloom. A woman was kneeling there clutching a cloak around her thin body. The sound I heard were her teeth chattering.

"She's fallen!" I exclaimed, and moved to help her

rise. My boots crunched on something. I gasped in horror. I knew that sound. I reached down to be sure. "Gravel!" I choked, appalled. My mother had made me kneel on gravel whenever I burnt the porridge or other household failures. "Whatever has she done to deserve such cruel punishment!" I demanded sharply of the abbess, shocked.

"She loved her daughter more than she loved God," she said with satisfaction.

Outraged, I reached to help the woman to her feet. But the abbess's talons cut into my arms with unexpected force. Her henchmen hustled us down a dark passageway and into a cell. I caught a glimpse of two stone benches covered in a thin layer of straw before the door slammed and a key scraped in the lock.

"She has locked us in!" gasped my employer. The old lady began to shriek. I threw myself towards the open window but the shutters slammed shut in my face. I heard the unmistakeable sound of a bar dropping into brackets. The old lady shrieked louder.

"Don't move. I have a light." I felt for the leather pouch on my belt where I keep a small box with flint wrapped in dry wool and a bit of straw. Lighting the morning fire had been my task since I was a child. The wool flared up and I fed a straw into the tiny flame. By this fragile light, my employer twisted more straw into a small torch. Now I saw that the shutters had a wide gap between them.

"I will slide my knife between those panels and lift off the bar," I whispered.

My employer's voice held panic. "No! How would

we get out of the convent?"

"At least we could bring that poor woman out there in here to stay warm."

"There are only two beds. Surely the abbess will return her to her cell for the night. If she stays there, she will freeze to death."

I reluctantly agreed. I made a thicker straw torch and by its quivering light we finished off our dried apricots. Then we wrapped ourselves in our cloaks and lay down on the cold stone ledges. I clasped Saint Thekla in my hand and wrapped my arms around the old lady. Oddly, I felt secure in our locked-in state.

Sometime later, I awoke. Someone was in our room. I opened my eyes. Above me hovered a white blur. It hung there, then dissolved slowly like millet flour dissolves in water. Strangely, I felt neither surprise nor fear. The old woman rested quietly in my arms so I went back to sleep, grateful for the respite from her terrors.

Morning light outlined the crack between the shutters. I slid my knife blade upward between them and the bar tumbled off. I pushed them open. A light breeze brought the sharp scent of the pine trees outlined against a grey dawn sky. The kneeling woman was still there. She had slumped sideways on the frost-coated stones. Horrified, I leapt out to help her. I touched her shoulder, then crossed myself with trembling hand.

"She has died!" I whispered to my employer who was watching from the window. "The poor woman perished alone while we slept so near! I will report this to the fort commander! This is murder!"

But before I could move, the abbess was behind me,

silent as her tethered hawk. She dug her talons into my arm. In an instant, I pressed my blade to her scrawny throat. A line of blood appeared. I pressed harder.

"You murdered this poor woman!" I hissed. "The commander will throw you in prison and cut off your head!"

Her cackle raised the hair on my neck. Her breath was so foul that I turned my face away. "The commander doesn't care," she laughed. "Neither does the bishop. He won't come even to give last rites."

"Then I will carry out your punishment!" I forced her onto her knees. Her blood would have wet the gravel had not my employer cried out.

"Thekla! My mother will not awaken!"

Indeed, the old lady had gone to her maker. The white blur that I had seen was her departing soul. I carried her frail body to the gate and laid her on the ground. My employer wept beside her while I ran to find Elias. A guard pointed to the office of the commander.

"Tell him to come out," I ordered.

He leered at me. "What will you give me?"

"Brother Elias! Brother Elias!" I shouted.

The door flew open and he hurried out, spilling what smelled like wine from the steaming tin cup in his hand.

"Brother Elias," I said, loudly. "Tell the commander that there are two dead women in that God-forsaken convent. The old woman who was in my care died last night in God's Grace. The other was foully murdered by that shit-souled skatopsychi abbess. She forced the poor soul to kneel on gravel all night. She died alone in the dark. Tell the commander that we need a coffin

43

to take the old woman to Amorion with us. The other woman needs a burial and justice. He must execute that murderous abbess before she kills more of those poor souls!"

Elias glanced over his shoulder. "This is not our affair, Despina Thekla," he said loudly. "I will ask for a coffin so we can take the old woman to Amorion. But I cannot tell the commander how to govern his fort."

I took the cup of wine from his hand and drank it down. The sweet warmth filled me with strength. I fixed him with a stern eye and spoke loudly. "What kind of holy man are you, Brother Elias, to turn away from a poor soul who was cruelly murdered by an abbess who was supposed to be her protector? A monk cares for the souls of the tormented. May God punish you for your failure of compassion."

"I'll do what I can," Elias muttered, snatching back the empty mug. "Go to your employer before the abbess goes after her, too."

"She wouldn't dare. I marked her throat with my knife. I'm waiting here."

"May the saints help me," he scowled and closed the door behind him.

I heard them speaking in that strange tongue. Then Elias opened the door and beckoned me inside. The commander was seated behind a desk eating a bowl of steaming porridge and drinking what smelled like mountain tea. He ran his eyes over me, then crooked his finger for me to move closer.

I don't move when men beckon. The commander glanced at the guard. A blow in my back flung me forward to the desk. Brother Elias did not move. The commander addressed me in his oddly accented Greek.

"I regret the death of your companion. I will send over a coffin. As for the nun who has perished, the Office of the Eparch of the Monasteries oversees monastic discipline. Take your complaint to their office in Amorion. I will see that she is buried. Otherwise the abbess will throw her body outside the gates and let the foxes scatter her bones. She has done this before, may God be her judge."

"I will indeed report this," I said stiffly. "But why do you wait for God's judgement? A commander has authority to punish the crimes in his fort. If you do not remove her, she will murder the other poor women in that convent."

He nodded. "The abbess is indeed a blight on humanity. However, she provides a roof for women who have no other refuge. I tolerate her for that. I will give her a warning."

I didn't believe him but I thanked him and turned to go. My eye was caught by a large parchment hanging on the wall. It had a curious coloured drawing. I went over to have a look. "What's this?" I asked over my shoulder.

"A map of the empire." The commander came to stand by me and placed his finger on the map. "Can you read? These large letters say 'Roman Empire of the East'. Our fort is here. This line is the road you came on. Here is Amorion."

I carefully spelled out the names. The only words I had ever seen were in Father Damianos's Rule of Saint Basil. Entranced by the colourful map, I didn't notice that the captain had moved closer. His hand slid between my legs. The point of my knife quickly pricked his throat.

"Move your hand or lose your blood!" I said evenly.

Brother Elias murmured something in a humorous tone in that odd language. The commander's hand left my crotch. I sheathed my knife.

The commander gave me a long look. "A word of advice, young woman. Be very cautious whose throat feels your knife."

"May you have a long and prosperous life," I said. "It would be a great kindness if you sent over something for my employer to drink and eat."

I returned to my employer who was sobbing over her mother's body at the convent gate. Elias appeared and handed me two tin cups of steaming mountain tea and a loaf of warm olive bread. My employer quickly devoured all of it. The two wine merchants staggered out of the barracks. Soldiers brought a coffin. We got the old lady into the box and I folded her hands over her silver cross. Elias sketched a cross in the air and muttered something which I could barely hear, much less understand. The soldiers hammered down the lid. As our coach rumbled out the gates with the old lady riding peacefully on the roof, I saw soldiers hacking out a trench in the graveyard.

The three other coaches in our caravan were waiting inside a small fort. The passengers were not yet ready, so my employer and I waded into the river and scrubbed ourselves with sand. I drew the back of my tunica forward between my legs and tucked it into the front of my belt like when I work in the fields. The water was icy but

I was desperate to rid myself of the stench of that awful convent. My employer had been weeping ever since we started out and she was drained of strength. She went to lie down in the coach. Elias sat on the bank and watched me scrub.

"You are lucky the commander didn't have your head off for pulling your knife on him," he commented. "You should curb your temper."

I exploded. "You laughed! Do you think I am a whore to be so treated?"

"If I had rebuked him, you and I both would be in a cell. Or dead. He is the law in that fort and he can do whatever he wants with impunity."

I didn't know what impunity meant so I kept scrubbing my legs. After a while I said, "How is it you speak the language of the Caliphate?"

"I was once a garrison commander on the Caliphate border. Officers along the empire's borders are required to speak the border languages."

"What about him?"

"He was a mounted archer in the Caliphate. He got captured and sold as a slave."

"He doesn't look like a slave now," I snapped, still angry at the encounter.

"He converted to Orthodoxy so his owner had to free him. The law says that Romans cannot own Roman citizens as slaves. He joined the army of Anatolia. It's a tradition from early Roman times. Captured soldiers can convert and join our army. Our own soldiers do the same sometimes. This commander is lucky to be alive. Emperor Constantine had a lot of Bulgar captives

47

beheaded. Captives are a nuisance. They have to be guarded and fed. And castrated. Eunuchs get a better price in the slave market."

I knew what a eunuch was. Once, in the Ikonion market, my mother had pointed at a fat bald man. "He's a eunuch. They cut off his balls like we cut off a ram's so he gets docile."

"That commander was no eunuch," I said to Elias.

Chapter III

My employer began sobbing in relief at our first glimpse of the stone walls of Amorion rising up a tall hill. Before we reached it, though, we had to pass two cemeteries, a stinking abattoir, and a foul-smelling tannery dumping waste into a river. Then came a maze of lanes and the smoking fires of pottery kilns and smithies. A smith was hammering out a sword.

Soldiers watched us from atop the wall towers as we rumbled over the wooden drawbridge; the moat was filled with garbage. The two sets of iron-studded gates were staggered so tightly that our coach could barely negotiate the turn. We pulled up in front of a pandohion on a tree-shaded plateia and Elias helped my employer out while I managed by myself, as usual, and looked around. There were four pandohia and as many kapelaria, as well as two stone churches and some wealthy looking houses. Meat was cooking somewhere over a grill. My mouth watered. I had eaten nothing all day.

A thick-bellied innkeeper hurried out. He bowed low to my weeping employer and bellowed at his servants to lift down the trunks and the coffin. I heard an older man who was scuttling down a steep lane calling out her name, tripping over his green tunica and long sleeveless skaramaggion. He must have been watching for the coach and had spotted the coffin. He led her off, both weeping, after he ordered his servants to carry the coffin to a church.

Elias and the pandoheus were pounding each other and bellowing out the rude names that men use when they are happy to see each other. His wife, I assumed she was the pandokissa, bustled out wiping her hands on her apron and beaming like her face would split. Her short thick legs in brown knotted stockings stuck out below her tunica. When they had all wiped away their happy tears, Elias beckoned me with a jerk of his head.

I dipped my head and knees. I didn't move closer. I smelled worse than I looked. The pandoheus and pandokissa ran their eyes over my torn tunica, mud-encrusted boots, and matted hair. The pandokissa shook her head. Elias beckoned me again. I edged closer.

"Despina Thekla, I've explained to my dear old friends that you were employed to care for that poor old grandmother. Unfortunately she died." He crossed himself piously and placed his hand on his heart. Everyone did the same. He continued. "I've explained that you need temporary work until your father and your brothers come to fetch you."

I dropped my eyes in what I hoped was a modest and humble manner. "Good Despina, please forgive how I look. My belongings were misplaced in Filomelion."

"Can you cook?" asked the pandoheus.

"My mother trained me well," I lied. I couldn't stir porridge without burning it.

The pandoheus slid Elias a sideways look. "I do need kitchen help. The assistant cook just left."

The wife shook her head vigorously. "She's told you a story, Brother Elias. She looks like a whore and I don't allow that in our inn."

"My employer will give me a good reference, Pandokissa," I replied with a sweet smile. She had to. I had seen her swilling wine and staggering to bed dead drunk.

The pandoheus shrugged. "Go scrub up at the bathhouse. It's women's day. Find some clean clothes. I'll give you a try."

The shrill scolds of the pandokissa followed Elias and me up the steep lane to the small wooden bathhouse.

"Here's where we part, Thekla. I have to make a side trip. I'll be back in a month or so. You are safe here. My friends run a respectable establishment. There's a small convent at the top of the town. You can sleep there. Your meals you'll take at your work."

"You're leaving?" I blurted. To my surprise, my heart lurched. I got control of it. "Then it's goodbye, Brother Elias. I won't see you again. I'm going on to Constantinople after I earn enough money for the coach."

"If you can control your temper and don't get yourself sacked. I advise you, go home to Ikonion. You won't find your soldier in Constantinople."

"I'm not going home," I said. "My father will make me marry the bone-scraper. I'll find Myri in Constantinople and I'll make him marry me. Or say he won't."

"And if he won't?"

"I'll cross that bridge when I get there."

He hesitated, like he was going to say something, then he turned and went up the hill. I watched him until he turned the corner, then I stepped cautiously into the bathhouse.

Ikonion had a bathhouse but I had never been in it. We washed in the river in nice weather and in a basin before the fire when it was cold. So I didn't know what to expect. The small outer room was pleasantly warm. I hung my cloak on a hook next to some others and put my boots under it. The valanissa took one of my silver milaresia and gave me a handful of copper folles in change. She lifted the curtain and waved me into a warm steamy room. I stepped in and stopped dead. Women naked as the day they were born were sitting on towels on the stone floor chatting while attendants poured steaming water over them from wooden buckets. They refilled them from brass spigots in the wall.

I turned to run but two attendants had got their hands on me and before I knew it, they had stripped off my tunica and underclothes and dunked them in a tub of steaming water. Then I was sitting on a towel on a warm stone floor while one valanissa poured warm water over my head and the other scrubbed me with a chunk of dried marrow that she squeezed full of warm water. She got a lot of skin along with the dirt. My hair took some scrubbing but by then I didn't care, I was so warm and tingling. I could have sat there all day.

"Such nice thick hair and a lovely chestnut colour,"

one valanissa commented cheerfully as she combed it out. "And a pretty face too."

I shrugged. "I've only seen my face in a bucket of water."

"Well, find a mirror, sweetie. Every woman should know her own face, especially one so pretty. You're from Ikonion, I'm guessing by your accent."

They got my story out of me, including that I had no clothes now that my tunica was under water.

"No worries, sweetie," said the other valanissa, "A traveller died and left a tunica and trousers and under-clothes. You can have them. And some advice: cover your hair and mouth when you're in the streets. Amorion is full of soldiers and travellers. You don't want them to think you're heteria."

"And don't let the pandoheus catch you alone," the other added. "He goes after pretty girls."

I shrugged. "I can handle him. It's the pandokissa I'm worried about. She doesn't like me and I need the work."

"She's jealous because you're pretty and she knows the pandoheus will go after you. Put him in his place and she'll have a heart of gold."

The borrowed clothes were loose but they would do. I paid for having my filthy clothes laundered which took another follis of my precious coins. Panic struck. What if I didn't get the job? How long before I died far from home like the Ikonion soothsayer in the pig market had predicted? But an odd feeling came over me. I had earned two milarisia. I could earn more. And the young monk soothsayer in Filomelion had said I would rise as high as an empress. Already I felt taller. Stronger. And cleaner.

The good feeling stayed with me as I asked the way to the Office of the Eparch of the Monasteries. It sat at the entrance to a monastery at the top of the town. A monk wearing a greasy brown tunica stinking of sweat and garlic barely lifted his nose from his soup. "A monk has already reported the abuse."

"It's murder, not abuse. What are you going to do about it, Brother?"

He slurped his tin cup of wine. "Not that I need to tell you, but we have itinerant agents who travel incognito as monks. They stay at monasteries and check that abbots aren't eating and drinking better than the monks. Or sleeping warmer. Like that." His lips twitched in a patronizing sneer. "Incognito means disguised. Itinerant means moving place to place."

"And how would an itinerant monk get his incognito self inside the walls of a convent where men aren't allowed? Do you even inspect convents, Brother krasopatera?"

"Not usually."

"Tell you what," I snapped. "I'll pretend I'm an incognito itinerant nun and I'll go visit that shithole and haul that stinking skatopsychi in here for you to talk to about how she makes nuns die on their knees. And I'll bring her nuns along so they can get warm and share your soup. And then I'll bring them over to your bishop."

"I'll take it under advisement." His eyes twitched towards the monastery door.

"The person who reported this, where is he staying?" I demanded.

"How should I know?"

Outside in fresh air, I spotted the small convent that Elias had recommended. The abbess was welcoming. She showed me the hospice where the nuns cared for ill or injured women. The cell she assigned me had a wool-stuffed mattress wrapped in clean linen and topped with a thick wool blanket. There was a niche where Saint Thekla could spend the night. And the narrow window looked over red tile roofs spread out at my feet like a gleaming red blanket. Window glass flashed in the sun. Amorion was a rich city—no wonder it was besieged by robbers, raiders from the Caliphate, and tax collectors. I had heard that fifty years before, eight hundred Amorion soldiers and imperial troops had held out against a Caliphate army of eight thousand. I could see why the residents wouldn't surrender this lovely town.

The pandohion and kapelarion were both already hopping with custom. The heavyset cook, dripping with sweat, pointed at a pot of boiling water. "Scoop those snails out with that slotted spoon, rinse off the snail snot in that bucket, and slide them back into the boiling water. And don't break them."

After that, I had to drain them and slide them into a big fry pan sizzling with pork fat. Cook tossed in sprigs of rosemary and a splash of vinegar which got me well spattered with hot fat. I swiped a snail when he wasn't looking and sucked out the flesh. Soft and tender! At home, my mother boiled snails once and we had to crack them with the back of a spoon and dig out the chewy things with the point of our knives.

Cook had a short temper but he was a kind man at

heart and right away he figured out I didn't know the first thing about cooking. Soon he was teaching me how to fry pork chops so they stayed tender. And roll out flat-bread and lay it on the curved iron bowl over the coals, wetting my hands to turn each piece without burning my fingers.

That night, warm in my convent bed, I listened to the spring rain drumming the tiles like a hundred running mice. I smiled at Saint Thekla in her niche. "I feel light, my heart and my whole body. And relaxed in a way I never knew. I'm not listening for my father's rough foot-fall coming to boot me out of bed or for sheep moaning in the night or the dog barking. In Ikonion, my days were always the same except for the weather. My future was Myrizikos and more of the same. Now each hour will be different."

My days began at dawn. I rose to the brass bell in the monastery ringing Orthros prayers and skidded down the mist-slippery cobblestone lanes to the kapelarion. I blew the fire embers into flames or lit it with my tinder, if cook hadn't banked them properly. I washed onions and leeks in the courtyard and chopped them and the garlic the way cook wanted before adding them to the fragrant, bubbling stews of rabbit or chicken or even mutton. The work was no harder than farm work and I was earning my keep in coins, which gave me a proud feeling. Then one day, as expected, the pandoheus beckoned me to-wards the back door.

"Let's see how you kill the chickens and rabbits for tonight's stew," he leered, pushing his leg against mine and forcing me out the back door.

I had my knife out before the door had slammed behind us. "Back away," I said with a cheerful smile, pointing the knife at him. "You don't want to get blood all over you when I chop off these heads, do you?"

I got two of the fowls by the legs before they could squawk and lined up their necks over the blood-stained stump that was obviously there for that purpose. "My brothers taught me how to use a knife," I explained sweetly. "It comes in handy when men don't know where to put their hands. Wait over there so the blood doesn't spurt on you."

While the chickens were bleeding out, I knocked the rabbits' heads together sharply before they knew what was coming. I skinned them, head to toe, which is easy once you know the trick of it. The pandoheus's face went a few shades lighter. He went inside.

After that, the pandokissa stopped scowling at me. Cook taught me how to boil, fry, and coddle eggs in cream in the ashes of the oven. And how to rub bulgur wheat together with sour milk and dry it in the outdoor oven to make trahana. We used it to thicken soups and stews. He showed me how to make it more tasty with mushrooms and spices I never knew existed, like fenugreek and cardamom. I made oxygala cheese by pouring raw buttermilk into a sheepskin and shaking it for days in the courtyard while it fermented.

But mostly I was hustling platters and jugs to tables because the pandoheus noticed that the tables filled up faster when I was passing around my smile and cheerful retorts. I kept quiet about myself and hoped that no one from Ikonion would come through and pass the word

57

to my father and brothers. Only once did my knife fly into my hand and that was when a patron put his hand between my legs, an event that raised a lot of laughter and never happened again. Like Elias had said, it was a respectable establishment and even though heteria did wander in looking for trade, those who were too obviously attracting men got kicked out by the pandokissa. The nicely dressed ones, she let in but they had to go somewhere else to make their money, not upstairs in the rooms.

I liked these women. We sat on the back steps and shared stories. One girl was from Ikonion. Her father had sold her to a pornovoskos, a girl-shepherd, but she said her life was easier than in Ikonion. She told me she washed her womb with alum after she left a man, to keep from making a child. If she did get with child, she used certain herbs. She gave me some alum and a packet of herbs and explained how to use them. Some she made into a brew to drink, others she soaked in water like a poultice and stuffed inside her. "You never know when you might need them, sweetie," she warned. She was right and I never forgot her kindness.

Table talk was mostly about Emperor Constantine's campaign. The soldiers from Amorion were full of battle stories. Everybody loves gossip, the worse the better, and I drank it like strong wine. They told how Emperor Constantine has heteria lined up outside his tent and he plants his seed in the most beautiful. They spoke with awe about how he swings his sword like a young man and sets up fake ambushes and retreats so that our soldiers could defeat the enemy without getting killed.

They loved him and were loyal to him, which they had to be anyway, the older ones pointed out, because he had made the army vow loyalty to him and his descendants and also vow never to venerate icons.

Every night, someone trotted out how Emperor Constantine had no sooner placed the crown on his head after his father died than his brother-in-law raised an army against him. Two years they battled, with the men of Amorion fighting for Emperor Constantine. Finally he trapped his brother-in-law inside Constantinople and starved him out. He had him blinded and locked inside a monastery with his wife and sons. The other big traitor, he had his head cut off and hung from the Arch of the Milion for three days. The Milion was a building in Constantinople where all roads in the empire began, they said. I thought about that. I would find the Milion as soon as I got to Constantinople. There my new life would begin.

Somebody always brought up how when Emperor Constantine was being born in the Great Palace in Constantinople in a room that was all purple, his father Leon the Isaurian had stood on the sea walls fighting off the Caliph's navy. Just when all seemed lost, a storm blew the enemy ships away from the walls. Which was a sign that God had sent the Isaurians to keep us safe.

I had only heard my father's curses at Emperor Constantine. Now I saw that Emperor Constantine was as beloved by his soldiers as Saint Thekla was to me. I mentioned to the innkeeper about my family being forced off their land near the Caliphate border and he said that the Caliph had done the same to his own people to make the No Man's Land, that it was an agreement between the two rulers. He said that moving people was nothing new, that Emperor Constantine's father had done it when he was emperor, and Emperor Constantine had shipped the people of some islands in the Aegean Sea to Constantinople after the plague had emptied out the city.

I heard stories about Emperor Constantine's oldest son, Co-Emperor Leon; how men laughed that he was 'weak' and that when the Emperor sent heteria to Leon's tent, they left disappointed. And about the Emperor's two oldest sons by Empress Evdokia, Christoforos and Nikiforos, they said they strutted around like they were already emperor and that when Emperor Constantine died, Leon would have another civil war on his hands.

Once in a while, the pandokissa gave me time off and I explored Amorion. It was the largest and richest city in Anatolia, she said, and I believed it by the number of shoppers and stores. Shop windows were stuffed with colourful ceramic bowls, shining copper vessels, and tapestries woven with birds and flowers. I ventured into a fabric shop and bought some undyed linen for a summer tunica and underclothes. I paid a raptaina to make it, and the pandokissa embroidered a panel for the front that was all flowers. One day, when I was gazing at a green glass necklace in a shop window, the shopkeeper beckoned me inside.

"Try on the necklace, omorfia mou, pretty girl. You will feel beautiful wearing it. Or how about a mother-of-pearl ring from the Red Sea? An amber pendant from Persia?"

My feet took me in like he was pulling them, and before I could say no, the necklace was around my neck and I was gazing into his polished silver mirror. I was shocked. I saw large dark eyes, a straight nose and full red lips. Chestnut hair curled thick around an oval face.

The shopkeeper smiled. "You're not the first girl to try on my jewellery just to look in my mirror. More lads are going to the kapelarion because of you, did you know? Buy the necklace. I'll give you a good price if you tell the travellers you found it here."

My fingers fumbled out the coins and the necklace was tied into my scarf—treasure like I had never known. Other exploring brought me to a winery, a leather workshop that made fine kid gloves, and an olive press to make oil from the few olive trees that managed to grow there. I watched parchment makers scrape sheep and goat skins to make vellum as soft as my own skin. I saw blocks of glass get melted down into tiny bottles for perfume and ointment.

One day, I came upon a small shrine on a steep lane. A crude cross was chiselled on the back wall of a shallow cave where seeping water had filled a small pool. A flat stone in front of the pool held the print of a woman's boot. A woman passing by told me that Saint Thekla's boot had pressed into the stone when she had refreshed herself there. She asked if I knew her story. Of course I did, being that Saint Thekla was the patron saint of Ikonion and I was named for her.

Saint Thekla had been engaged to a wealthy man. When Saint Pavlos came through Ikonion preaching chastity, Saint Thekla took his advice to heart. This got her tied to the stake and Saint Pavlos thrown in prison. They escaped together. Saint Pavlos went on to Rome. Saint Thekla travelled alone for years, healing sick people. Finally she came to Rome and lay down beside the grave of Saint Pavlos to die. This very spot was where my name saint had placed her foot. That meant that I was following her path.

Cautiously, I placed my boot where hers had stood. A perfect fit. I stood there for a long time, overwhelmed by how alike we were. I, too, was fleeing Ikonion and heading for a big city. I, too, was on my own and fighting off assault-minded men. Right then, I knew I was on the right path. I would find Myrizikos and we would be wed. Which goes to show that what you think is the right path one day can be completely different when you actually step on it.

Months passed and I rubbed elbows with thick-bearded merchants from beyond the Pontus Sea who taught me a bit of their heavy Rus language. I served rich people, monks, priests, and Jews who brought their own food. Some slaves captured in the Caliphate taught me their curse words. There were lots of eunuchs, mostly servants or slaves, but some who were wealthy merchants or soldiers. My heteria friends told me the difference between the eunuchs.

"Some eunuchs have their balls cut off by their families when they are infants or children because these kind of eunuchs are calm, placid and in demand as servants, so making their child a eunuch would guarantee work. They have hardly any hair and high voices, and tend to be fat. Other eunuchs have their balls cut off when they are adults, usually war prisoners to be sold as slaves. They still like to lie with women, so you can enjoy yourself and not get with child." They all laughed.

One late morning in July, after I had been working two months, I had finished scrubbing the fry pan and had come out to sweep the eating room. The pandokissa was at a table by the window with a stack of wax tablets in front of her, also papyrus pages, a quill box, and a bottle of ink. She was cursing. I edged closer. The wax tablets were covered with words and numbers. She glared at me.

"Shut up that racket! I can't hear myself think!"

"I'm good at sums, can I help?" This was not a lie. Father Damianos taught girls and boys until age eight. Girls stopped learning then. But I was good at sums so Father Damianos lent me a wax tablet to practice. I also copied his Rule of Saint Basil to learn to spell.

The pandokissa flung up her hands. "My idiot husband isn't careful with numbers. I can't make sense of this mess! The tax collector will rob us blind if I can't show what comes in."

"Heaven forfend!" I pulled up a stool. After some study, with her cursing her husband and me writing columns on the papyrus, we straightened out the mess. The work calmed me and gave me a rest from the kitchen. I was proud to see my letters and numbers lined up straight and accurate. After that, we sat every few days and did the accounts. She gave me an extra folles, and after that she stopped asking why my father and brothers hadn't come for me, or even written.

We were well into September when two imperial messengers climbed off the mail coach and took a room. The pandoheus himself served them supper. Pretty quickly, he was passing on the news. Empress Evdokia was putting on a bride show for her step-son, Co-emperor Leon. This would be the first imperial wedding since Emperor Constantine married Evdokia sixteen years before. The messengers wanted a parade of beautiful young women between fourteen and sixteen from wealthy families. The loveliest would go to Constantinople to the bride show.

Soon, rich men and their daughters were jamming the kapelarion. A couple of travelling merchants eating in the corner were laughing. I asked them why.

"Everyone in Constantinople knows that Empress Evdokia has arranged for her niece to win the contest. Nothing is ever as it seems in the Great Palace."

I personally wasn't impressed by the best that Amorion had on offer and neither were the messengers because they left without sending anyone to Constantinople. The days were getting shorter and the nights had gone cold. Soon it would be winter and the road to Constantinople would be impassable. Either I had to buy a coach ticket or stay in Amorion until spring. The trouble was, I couldn't find a caravan that would accept a single young woman travelling alone. Single women were heteria. Then in walked Brother Elias wearing a reasonably clean monk's tunica. I grinned like a fool at his handsome face.

"Where have you been?" I demanded. "You said you were coming back in a month."

"Dear Cousin, does it matter what mud my boots have collected since we parted? The future is our concern. I must depart for Constantinople and so must you, unless you have decided to wed a good Amorion lad." He took one look at my scowl and laughed.

"No? Well then, a caravan of rug merchants is leaving this week under full armed guard. For one silver milaresion, you and I can ride inside a wagon to Dorylaion. Fix your thoughts on the great cities on our path: Nicaea, Nikomidia, Pendykion, Chalkidon. We will see the imperial warhorses in Malagina. We will sail the Propontis Sea and enter the Golden Gate into Constantinople."

My head whirled with excitement but then tremors hit my stomach at the thought of leaving Amorion. I had made the town my home. And suspicion struck. I narrowed my eyes.

"You're a man. You can travel alone. Why do you want me along? I'm not heteria."

He put a hand on his heart. "We are simply two travellers with a common destination. You will be a nun and I will be your cousin, Brother Elias."

"Are you really a monk? The truth, now," I demanded.

"Why does it matter?" he smiled. "Let us step onto the road together and enjoy the pleasure of each other's company."

I still wondered why he wanted the company of a woman. But what could I do but laugh at his silly words, I was so happy to see him again.

Chapter IV

My employers wept when I left but my eyes were dry. The pandokissa's sister had started pointing out likely husbands for me. She had even made me an amulet to attract a husband and the pandokissa had made me wear it. I took it off with relief. I fastened my purse, plump with my hard-earned coins, onto the leather strap around my neck and tossed my satchel and thick winter cloak in the wagon. All I owned was in it: two tunicas, underclothes, sandals, and a papyrus bearing a testimony praising my work at the inn. I had written the lavish praise myself and my employers were pleased to sign. I stepped out beside Elias, happier to walk than ride. My legs felt the pleasure of movement—they wanted to run! My heart soared like the hawks drifting above us. Soon I would be a stratiotis, the wife of a soldier!

Our caravan kept to the stone military road except

when our scouts led us onto older roads that were soft earth and easier on the knees of our mules and on our backsides. The Great Alexander had passed this way as he conquered his way east, Elias told me. We crossed ourselves as we skirted deserted stone villages that Elias said had been emptied by the plague. The first evening, we stopped inside a fortified town surrounded by a high wall. I turned my steps toward a convent with the other women but Elias drew me down a side lane.

"Save your coins, Cousin Thekla. We'll sleep in the hay for nothing."

Indeed, an ostler gave us soft beds in the hayloft above his stables. While he and our wagoneers lifted the harnesses off the sweating mules, Elias went to find our supper. I climbed to the hayloft and fell asleep with my arms wrapped around our belongings. Walking beside a wagon was more tiring than riding in a coach. Elias woke me with a shout. He had acquired a grilled chicken wrapped in cloth, I didn't ask how. His tin kettle was chock full of marrow and turnips. The ostler brought out his garum fish sauce, the wagoneers laid out their barley bread and grapes, and we all tucked in. I ate myself full, relieved myself in an empty horse stall, and climbed back to the loft. October rain tapped on the slate roof. The mules gently blew hay dust from their soft noses, Elias and the other men were laughing at some ribald joke. I smiled as I covered myself with my cloak. I was warm, dry, and well-fed.

"What could be better?" I murmured to Saint Thekla securely knotted in the corner of my scarf. Elias's boots scraped on the ladder. The hay rustled near me. I moved

67

my hand to my knife but he was already snoring. The next night we slept again above stables. I skinned the three rabbits I had felled that day with stones from my sling and the ostler spit-roasted them over his fire. I fell asleep to Brother Elias snoring. I wished our journey would last forever.

The days passed wonderfully clear and sharply colder. We entered dark forests, followed rivers through narrow valleys, climbed steep mountains and forged streams. I spotted the kalamodytes bird plunging down reeds to snap up tiny fish. Larks with black throat markings pecked for grubs and seeds, and woodpeckers drummed alerts. I heard the silvery trill of a blue rock thrush and spotted the tiny red crowned fircrest disappearing into the trees in a flash of fire. What a beautiful place was our empire! My heart swelled with pride of belonging; I was a citizen of the Empire of the Romans of the East, travelling to Constantinople! Never had I felt so free. It was a lightness of spirit that I cannot describe and that I did not understand until it was gone.

Nakoleia was a large fortress and market town where the Amorion road met the north-south road to Dorylaion. I paid for a bed in a pleasant convent and left my satchel there while I scrubbed myself in the bathhouse. Elias went off to stay in a monastery, or so he said. Next morning, I went to the market to purchase bread for my mid-day meal. I felt rested and content, full of lentil soup and barley bread for supper, and breakfast of lightly beaten eggs fried with goat cheese and topped with heavy slices of millet porridge. I spotted Elias coming out of the army barracks, an odd place for a monk to sleep. I tracked him through the market. Had my eyes not been fixed upon him, I would have missed his left hand scooping up an apple and lump of cheese while his right hand blessed the beaming vendors.

I confronted him when we were on the road. "Monks don't sleep in army barracks. Or steal. And where is the shaved spot on your head where you were tonsured? You never pray in churches. You don't even bless your bread. You know more about the chariot races in the Hippodrome than a monk who took vows of poverty. You're not a monk."

He clasped his hands and bowed his head piously. "Sins of commission and omission. I will pray for forgiveness. And find a barber."

"I told you my story, now tell me yours," I demanded.

He gazed at the clouds as if deciding from which to pluck his tale. "Let us say that two years ago, I was working for the Office of the Eparch of the Monasteries."

"Aha! You reported the murderous abbess to the office in Amorion, I knew it."

"How quick you are. I left that employment due to a small problem with the imperial authorities which I won't go into. My superiors sent me to a monastery in Seflukia. It is the port for Antioch."

I narrowed my eyes suspiciously. "Your superiors sent you into the Caliphate? Did they want you to die?"

"That idea did occur to me. However, there is a community of Christians living in Antioch. Merchants use the port of Seflukia. I lived in the monastery and cooked and scrubbed floors for travellers. Seflukia has a shrine to Saint Thekla of Ikonion, I spent much time before it in pious contemplation," he added piously.

"Saint Thekla is my saint! She is the icon that I carry," I exclaimed, surprised.

"I wondered if that was the case, given that you come from Ikonion and you bear her name," he said. "At long last, I received word that the authorities were no longer concerned with me. So, I am returning to Constantinople, cautiously, to be certain of my welcome."

Dorylaion is an old Roman city with high walls that overlook a river. The innkeeper at a pandohion fell over himself with joy at the sight of Elias. Apparently they were old friends. I paid for a bed in the women's dormitory. For three pleasant nights, we rested and scrubbed ourselves and our clothing in the thermal springs. We ate in kapelaria where I greedily devoured mouth-watering stewed mutton or pheasant sealed in a clay pot with juniper berries and rashers of cured ham, then slow-cooked in the ashes of the fire all night.

"You should watch your funds," warned Elias. "Once we get near Constantinople, everything gets expensive."

"More reason to enjoy life now." I said, wiping my mouth on my sleeve. "I will find work in another kapelarion when I need money."

"And clean up your language," he added. "There's no need to lay a curse on everyone who annoys you. That goes for pulling out your knife, too. Control your temper, if you possibly can."

"You try being a woman and see how much you need your mouth and your knife," I snapped, spearing a chunk of lamb with my knife. "Although I suppose it won't hurt to learn some new words. Then I will sound like I had some learning besides the Rule of Saint Basil."

We left Dorylaion riding in a wagon of a military mule train transporting firewood to the fortress of Aigilon—fuel for the beacon flame tower. It was a steep slog up a mountain and the muleteer made us walk to ease the burden on his beasts. We arrived tired and footsore but in far better condition than the string of scrawny slaves who were chopping wood and carrying it up to a broad platform atop a stone tower. The pitiful souls were thinly dressed for the October mountain air.

"Wretched creatures," I murmured to Elias. "I wonder if they came from the Caliphate frontier. Maybe their guard knew Myrizikos."

Elias went to get us bunks inside the travellers' hut while I asked the guard.

"What do you care about that loser?" he leered, running his hot eyes over me. He moved closer. "Come on, sweetie, share my bunk. A silver milaresion for you."

I pulled out my knife. "Malakismeni! May leprosy get you!" I spat.

"Hey, our emperor never sleeps alone, why should I?" he called after me.

"A soft answer turneth away wrath," Elias quoted virtuously from outside the travellers' hut where he was scrubbing turnips in a bucket of water.

"Not where I come from," I snapped.

I skinned the two rabbits I had brought down with my sling that afternoon and hacked them into pieces. Elias took them inside the hut to boil into stew in his tin kettle. I threw the innards into the pig pen and gave the pelts to the army cook. When I got back, the stew was bubbling on the stove which was a heavy iron plate laid across large stones with a fire in between. I fed the flames with dried goat dung and added sprigs of rosemary and wild greens to the pot.

Suddenly there came over me a panic so great that I could not speak. This was the fear that troubled my sleep, what I had been not admitting to myself: I would never find Myrizikos. I would die alone far from home.

"Tell me where in Constantinople to find Myrizikos," I asked in a trembling voice.

Elias gave me a long look. He picked up a stick and drew a rough triangle in the dirt. He planted his stick near one corner. "Start here at Chalke Gate. It's the entrance to the Great Palace. Just inside are the barracks for the imperial guard, the Tagmata. Ask there."

His voice soothed me and I grew calmer. He drew lines across the triangle.

"Mesi Street, the main street of Constantinople. Starts at the Milion where all roads in the empire begin. Then it passes through the Forum of Constantine and other fora. A forum is what they call a plateia here. Everyone walks through the Forum of Constantine so try sitting there and watching the crowds. Mesi Street turns up Fourth Hill to the Church of Holy Apostles. The Emperor goes there to pray. Your lad might be guarding him there or at the Blachernae Church at Blachernae Palace on the far side of Constantinople. Or walk along the road that follows the outside of the land walls. There are nine gates. Ask the guards at the gates. Check out the military parade ground at the far end of the walls. Or walk seven miles to the parade ground and barracks at Evdomon Palace."

Too many names! Too many places! My panic returned. Just then, a merchant entered and Elias invited him and his slave to share our stew. He shared his cheeses and wine. Tomorrow he was returning to Nicaea, he said. We could ride in his wagon. The big news was that Empress Evdokia had birthed her fifth son.

"They are calling him Anthimos!" He raised his cup of wine. "Six sons now has our Emperor, Leon from his first wife and five more from Empress Evdokia. He's found a bride for Leon, I heard in Nicaea. Some girl from Athens. He's stashed her at Hieria Palace until the betrothal ceremony."

"Is she in the bride show?" I asked.

He laughed. "The Emperor cancelled the bride show."

He and Elias merrily toasted our emperor's loins with ribald jokes. The wine made me sleepy so I wrapped myself in my cloak and curled up on the bunk I would share with Elias in this communal sleeping hut. Watching the firelight eased my panic. Elias lay down beside me. He moved closer. I started to reach for my knife. But his body blocked the draft and he started snoring. I let him stay.

The merchant's wagons moved quickly, as he had delivered his foodstuffs, and by afternoon we were camped by the broad and muddy Sangarius River. We slept inside the wagon and woke to a cold damp fog. We shared our paximadia rusks and dried figs for breakfast. All day, my breath mingled white with the fog that hovered over the slow silent river. Swans appeared and vanished leaving only a widening vee. Finally, we climbed a low range of hills and left the fog behind. I gazed at green pastures, thick vineyards, lush farm land, and gold and red autumn forests that flowed up Mount Olympus, Elias said. At its base lay a shining blue lake.

"Lake Askania and the fortress of Nicaea," said Brother Elias. "Where my dear auntie has soft beds for us. You are looking at the rich farms of Bithynia that feed the stomachs of Constantinople. And among them are the rich monasteries and convents that feed the wrath of our emperor because they won't stop painting icons."

Our wagons rattled up to the gates of Nicaea and our benefactor leapt out to identify himself to the guards. We climbed out and stretched our stiff limbs. I stared in amazement at the great city wall that rose straight from the lake.

"Lake Askania protects Nicaea from enemy siege engines," said Elias, ever informative. "Boats can bring in supplies by water. Twenty-seven years ago, Emperor Constantine's brother-in-law based his army here while he tried to take the throne. Emperor Constantine drove him out. Even these walls and the one hundred watch towers couldn't stop our emperor."

I pulled off my boots and waded my hot, sore feet into the cool water. Rapture! I cupped my hands and gulped the sweet water, then plunged in my head. "Get out of the water," Elias called irritably. "They're closing the gates."

Soldiers were patrolling between watch towers on two city walls, one inside the other. A shallow trough ran along the side of the street carrying all sorts of stinking wet filth. I smelled public toilets and went over to use them. They were a long slab of marble with holes in it, balanced over a stone trough. When I left, an attendant threw a bucket of water down the trough.

Immediately, I was lost in a maze of lanes and plateias and shops, churches and monasteries. Everywhere, banners and flags celebrated the birth of the Emperor's fifth son from Empress Evdokia. A zamnykistria played his three-stringed sambuca while the crowd tossed coins to five thymelikia who danced around him. The gate into Auntie Sofia's villa was on a narrow lane behind the Church of Holy Wisdom. A muscular eunuch wearing a blue and yellow tunica opened the gate into a wide courtyard. A short stocky woman wearing a flowing white tunica over loose white trousers and a scarlet scarf around her heavy neck came shrieking out of the house. She threw herself at Elias and didn't let go. He endured this patiently, rolling his eyes at me. Finally she noticed me and my dripping hair, wet tunica and filthy boots. Elias held up a hand to forestall her comment.

"Auntie Sofia, please welcome Sister Thekla. She is a nun travelling to Constantinople to tell her brother that her father has died."

I turned away to stifle my laugh at his lie. A movement caught my eye. In a pool in the middle of the courtyard, huge golden fish were swimming lazily over a picture of a woman. She was wearing nothing but a carefully draped white scarf. I looked closer. She was made of tiny glittering tiles in all colours of the rainbow that flashed in the sun.

"Those fish are carp," said Auntie Sofia, sharply. "We eat them. You'll feel much more comfortable in a convent, Sister. I'll have my eunuch take you. Don't forget your satchel."

Elias picked up his knapsack. "If she goes, I go."

"Don't be silly!" Auntie Sofia grabbed his arm. "I haven't seen you in two years, no news at all, even Leon said he didn't know where you went and he always knows where you are. Your mother and father have been frantic. You can't leave, just like that."

"I'm happy to stay in a convent, Brother Elias," I interrupted. "The holy sisters and I will remember your souls in our prayers before we dip our bread crusts in Saint's Broth."

"I'm fond of Saint's Broth, myself," he said grimly.

Auntie Sofia hung on tighter. "Sister whatever her name is welcome to stay. I only thought she would feel more comfortable with her own kind. Wait right there, Sister, I'll have my mizoteris find you something clean to wear."

"I have clean clothing, thank you, Auntie Sofia. What I need is a bath."

"Indeed you do need a bath, Sister. And you, Elias. Take her to the public baths. We'll have supper when you come back. I have so much to tell you. I have just come from visiting your dear parents. The gossip is shocking! Emperor Constantine has brought a little gold-digger from Athens to marry Co-emperor Leon! Poor Leon doesn't know what to think. He wants to talk to you. He even came to your parents' house and asked where you were. You two were such friends when you were children. I can't wait to write them that you are here!"

I stared at Elias. "You know the co-emperor?"

"When we were children." Elias turned me towards the gate.

On the way to the baths, I kept my eyes open for a convent, in case Auntie Sofia managed to kick me out. Every shop-keeper lounging in a shop door shouted out a welcome to Elias.

"No one is calling you Brother Elias," I noted.

"It's a recent development."

The gleaming marble bathhouse had separate entrances for men and women. The outer room reeked of jasmine. I paid the valanissa an exorbitant amount, left my boots on a shelf and ducked through the curtain.

And stopped, stunned. Bald eunuchs with hairless bodies naked to the waist were scrubbing naked women who lounged on tiled benches. The walls were shining white tiles painted with wondrous birds and flowers.

"I'll bathe in the lake!" I exclaimed in a hurry.

But the two valanissa were quick and soon they had me naked on a bench and a eunuch was dousing me with warm water while another eunuch scrubbed me and my hair with soft sponges. A third took my dirty feet in his hands and was skilfully scrubbing out the grime with pumice and kneading away the aches at the same time. It was a glorious bath and I walked out with my hair piled on my head, wearing my linen tunica with the flowers embroidered down the front, feeling like a new woman. And a barefoot one. I was carrying my dusty boots.

"The valanissa wouldn't let me put these on my clean feet," I complained to Elias who was outside, scrubbed and well-dressed in a linen tunica that no monk ever wore. I sniffed my arms and made a face. "I smell like heteria."

He stared at me. His mouth opened and closed. He stared at my bare feet, pointed to a bench by the door, and left. After a while, he returned carrying a pair of sandals. They had a spray of sparkling jewels over the arch.

"I can't afford these, Elias," I muttered, gazing hungrily at the beautiful things. "Besides, your Auntie Sofia thinks I'm a nun."

"Auntie Sofia thinks a lot of strange things. Wear them. They're a gift."

Auntie Sofia raised her plucked and hennaed eyebrows at me when we returned. Her mouth moved but nothing came out. Finally she found her voice. "Where ever did you take your vows, Sister Thekla?"

"Later," interrupted Elias firmly. "Now we need food and drink."

It was after dark by then. Auntie Sofie kept her suspicious eyes on me as we moved into a room with a rug woven with flowers so bright that even in the candlelight they seemed alive. We got comfortable on big cushions then two servants proceeded to bring in dish after dish. I had to ask what they were, I had never known such a feast! Chicken thighs grilled with cumin and caraway seeds and dripping with honey and sesame seeds, cabbage braised in wine, lightly fried cheese balls preserved in olive oil and spread on crunchy flat bread. We finished with fried curd balls doused in a syrup of honey and lavender water and dates stuffed with almonds. I tried to eat slowly, but I couldn't help gobbling it down.

Auntie Sofia didn't notice. Her fleshy cheeks wobbled as she chewed and talked.

"Irini of Athens," she reported. "That's the little invader that Emperor Constantine has brought to wed Leon. She's seventeen and still unmarried which tells you right away that something is wrong since nobody wanted her. For one thing, she's an orphan—certainly not a suitable consort for a co-emperor! Her parents died in a shipwreck or something. Worse—she's from Athens!" Auntie Sofia clanked her long necklaces of green stones set in silver in agitation.

"What's wrong with people from Athens?" I inquired, through full mouth.

"They're heathens and barbarians! They bow down before naked statues of the ancient gods and goddesses that are everywhere in the streets!"

Elias laughed. "Athenians don't bow before statues. And not all the statues are naked. I've been there."

Auntie Sofia ignored him. "She was raised in her uncle's house, an old friend of the Emperor's, apparently. He put her on Emperor Constantine's warship just like that, not even a chaperone, just some cousin. Surely the uncle knew what would happen on that ship. Everyone knows about the emperor. They were in Thessaloniki for some time. She was ill, the story goes." She lifted an eyebrow.

"Auntie, not every vicious rumour is true," Elias protested.

"The Emperor has installed her in Hieria Palace, dear. You know what that means."

"What's Hieria Palace?" I asked.

Elias answered. "It's a lovely stone palace across the Propontis Sea from Constantinople. Fifteen years ago, Emperor Constantine locked over three hundred bishops inside for six months until they decreed that it was heresy to pray before an icon. I told you about that before. Mostly, the Emperor uses Hieria Palace to meet his generals before a campaign. And foreign dignitaries."

"And his concubines!" Auntie Sofia burst out. "Obviously, he was planning to keep this girl there with his other women. But when he got to Constantinople, he discovered that Empress Evdokia had plans to marry Leon to her niece. Just like that, the Emperor decided that this Athens girl would wed Leon. Empress Evdokia is livid, your mother heard."

"As is the family of the niece, I imagine," commented Elias. "I wonder how much they slipped the empress to get their daughter on the throne."

Auntie Sofia sighed. "Poor Empress Evdokia. She worked so hard to find a suitable wife for Leon. And out of the goodness of her heart. He isn't her son, after all. He's from that pagan daughter of the Khazak khan, the one with the strange name."

"Tzitzak. She converted when she married Constantine, Auntie. Her Christian name was Irini."

"Married off to seal a treaty. A year later, she died in childbirth. Leaving us Leon who has his own problems, as you well know, my dear."

Elias gave her a sharp look but Auntie Sofia carried on.

"How Emperor Constantine got Leon betrothed to the daughter of the king of the Franks, no one knows. It got called off, anyway. Empress Evdokia had something to do with getting it, I heard. Now the empress has got to get rid of this Athens orphan. Otherwise, Emperor Constantine will die and we will be left with this nobody from Athens as empress, God help us." She jangled her gold and silver bracelets.

Elias threw back his wine. "Listen, Auntie, I will tell you why Empress Evdokia is so against this young woman. Evdokia has given the Emperor five sons and a daughter. None of them will ever become emperor because Emperor Constantine has named Leon as his successor. When Leon becomes emperor, this Athenian wife will follow tradition and kick Empress Evdokia out of the Palace. If Evdokia wants to continue living in Palace luxury, she has to get rid of this woman from Athens and marry her niece to Leon. How she will do that, I can't imagine."

Auntie Sofia sniffed. "At the moment, the empress can do nothing. She just gave birth so she is stuck in semi-isolation for forty days. That's until the end of November. The Emperor set the betrothal ceremony for the first week in November. I heard he's bringing this Athens woman across the Propontis Sea from Hieria Palace in a warship under silk sails, like she's some sort of high-level dignitary."

"What else have you heard about this Irini of Athens?" Elias motioned the eunuch to re-fill his wine cup.

"No-one has seen her except the sailors on the ship from Athens. She must be beautiful, if she caught the eye of our emperor." She waved her glass at the eunuch for more wine. "I don't care who marries Co-emperor

Leon, it's a big fancy wedding during the Brumalia wine festivities and Nativity season and there will be parties, parties, parties. I'm coming to stay with your parents. The priests in Nicaea won't allow anything but church ceremonies. They say the Brumalia is pagan. Thank Heavens for Emperor Constantine and his Brumalia drinking parties in Constantinople."

"I want to see this Irini of Athens," I said impulsively. I felt an odd kinship with this young woman. We were the same age. We had both left our towns to come to Constantinople to be wed. We both knew no one and had to start out alone.

Elias shrugged. "If we get to Hieria in time, we can watch her get on this silk-sailed warship. But don't count on it. First, I have to get to Malagina."

Suddenly I was so tired that I meekly followed the mizoteris to my room. She was a stern-looking woman with a bunch of keys jangling on her belt. We climbed a flight of stairs to a room with a lovely flowered carpet and a window overlooking the courtyard. I could hear Elias and Auntie Sofia arguing below. I would spend one night in this glorious villa and find a convent, I decided. I wouldn't stay where I wasn't wanted. I could find a caravan to take me to Constantinople from here. I put my satchel and boots in the cupboard, took off my tunica, and stretched out on the low bed.

Morning light and a delicious smell woke me. My stomach growled. My boots and the rest of my clothing had disappeared from the cupboard. Heart pounding, I searched frantically through my satchel for my scarf and for Saint Thekla securely tied in the corner. The scarf was gone. But my shaking fingers found Saint Thekla.

I clutched her to my heart, waiting for it to stop pounding. Should I leave the house before Auntie Sofia called the soldiers to come get me? No, I decided, forcing myself to be calm. Elias wouldn't allow her. I put on the tunica I had worn the night before and went down to the courtyard.

Elias and Auntie Sofia were eating szingi, small fritters doused with honey and nuts, and cooked apples sprinkled with kinammomon.

"I'll be moving to a convent when I get my clothes back," I announced.

"You're staying here," Elias said with a hard glance at his auntie. "Auntie Sofia wants to show you the sights of Nicaea."

***

"Where did Elias take his monk's vows?" I asked his auntie as we walked through the markets.

"Vows?" she exclaimed. "Elias took vows? I don't believe it! He had a perfectly good position with the Eparch of the Monasteries and he'll get another one, with his family connections."

I knew he wasn't a monk, I thought with satisfaction. What a liar that man is.

Priests and monks were everywhere. I had never seen so many churches. Auntie Sofia bought silk for a new tunica and silver bracelets in the quarter where the Jews lived and worked. She was showing me how rich she was. I acted unimpressed. I was sorry to leave that lovely villa the next day, especially Auntie Sofia's fabulous cook. I was even more sorry to backtrack instead of going on to Nikomidia and Constantinople.

"It's only one extra day on the road, " Elias jollied me as I sulked out Lake Gate where we had come in instead of Constantinople Gate on the other side of town. "You'll love watching the Emperor's beautiful war horses in the Malagina Valley. The armies meet the Emperor there when they leave on campaign to the eastern frontier."

A farmer took a copper follis to let us sleep in his hayloft that night. I stretched out on the sweet-smelling new hay and listened to rain rattle the roof tiles. I was barely a body's length from Elias. I smiled as I thought about how he had stared when I came out of the baths with my hair piled up on my head and reeking of jasmine. I smiled, thinking of the jewelled sandals inside my satchel. Myrizikos had never looked at me like that, or bought me anything in the Ikonion market. After I had lain with Myrizikos in the tall summer grass, I had thought to myself, is this why men lay with women? This sweaty struggle where I ended up face down?

Elias was still awake. Men are like goats. You can feel when they are restless. I turned towards him. The hay rustled and his arms were around me and my tunica was over my head and it wasn't a sweaty struggle at all. He pushed his tongue in my mouth and afterwards I held his smooth shaved cheeks against mine.

"Auntie Sofia said you would never take monk's vows," I whispered.

"You knew that all along."

I could feel him smile. He fell asleep. I slid my fingers around my tiny icon of Saint Thekla hidden in the corner of my scarf. "I just fornicated with a man who is not my betrothed and who lied about being a monk," I confessed to her, wanting to giggle. I breathed in the sweet scent of rain bringing the sky and the earth together and fell asleep in Elias's arms, a nice heavy sleep like the rain.

The next day, we climbed the cliff to the fortress that guarded the imperial stock farms in the Malagina Valley. Elias disappeared with some soldiers into a tunnel cut into the rock. My eyes traced the road we would follow to Nikomidia.

"A day's walk." A soldier put his hand on my waist. I slid out my knife. He stepped back with a resigned grin. He showed me a water collection cistern that he said the army of the Great Alexander had built, and the platform where the Great Alexander's huge catapults once stood.

Elias came back looking sombre and didn't speak all the way down to the pastures where beautiful mares and colts grazed and magnificent warhorses whistled and paced the fences. That night we slept body-to-body inside a forest cave, our first night outside a wall.

"Thieves don't venture this close to Malagina," Elias murmured. But my hand was on my knife hilt when I closed my eyes and it was still there in the morning.

We passed through fields smelling sweetly of beets, turnips, and great heads of cauliflower. The grain harvest was over and the fields stripped bare. The town of Nikomidia sat by the Propontis Sea. I couldn't take my eyes off so much water. It went clear to the horizon. I took off my boots and let the gentle waves wash my dusty legs. I plunged in my arms and flung cold water over my hot face and sweaty neck. I filled my cupped hands and

85

took a gulp.

"Salt!" I choked.

Elias was still laughing when we entered the gates, curse the man.

Nikomidia was a crowded smelly market city that reeked of fish and pisspots. Shallow troughs ran with filth along the streets. Every pandohion turned us away. "Imperial betrothal and wedding," was the story.

We searched until dusk, passing under three aqueducts and the palace where Emperor Constantine had fled from the plague in Constantinople. No convents or monasteries had beds for us, even the largest dedicated to the saints Pantaleon the All Compassionate and the great martyr Saint Barbara. An ostler found us space in his hayloft. I gave him half what he wanted and he took the coins with a grin. I forgave his thievery for he was a cheerful soul and let us grill the fish we had bought over his fire. We shared it with him.

"Every social climber is going to Constantinople for the royal wedding," he said. "If you make it to Hieria Palace by tomorrow, you'll see this Athens woman get on a warship for Constantinople. Under white silk sails." He dropped a lecherous wink.

I was glad to leave stinking Nikomidia and walk beside the sparkling Propontis Sea to Lybissa where the great Hannibal of Carthage had committed suicide, Elias said, whoever he was. We reached Pendykion fortress the next evening, our last night before Hieria Palace. And probably my last night sleeping next to Elias's warm body, I thought with deep regret.

Pendykion was a sizeable fort and way-station for the

imperial post. A tired pandoheus offered us an empty corner of his crowded stable loft and we were grateful for it. Our supper was on the beach, fish grilled over a fisherman's fire and mussels from his cookpot. Elias pointed to a string of islands not far away, soft green shadows on a silver sea.

"Prison islands. There are twelve monastery prisons on them, most built by the father of Emperor Constantine. Prisoners are too far from Constantinople to make trouble but near enough to be under his eye. Emperor Constantine exiled our previous patriarch, Patriarch Constantine, to the biggest island, Prinkypos. He accused the poor old man of conspiring to take the throne. Nineteen others were accused. One was Minister of the Imperial Post, the highest position in the government. Emperor Constantine had him blinded and exiled. One was commander of Thrace. Condemned to death. The army made such a stink about that that Emperor Constantine reduced his punishment to blinding and exile. Plus an annual flogging. The other conspirators were exiled to distant monasteries. Patriarch Constantine was in prison on Prinkypos Island for two years."

"Why would the Patriarch want the throne?" I asked. "He was already head of the church."

Elias's mouth twisted bitterly. "He was falsely accused. Certain priests were angry at him for changing his beliefs. He had been a monk and a bishop and a fervent believer in the sanctity of icons. When Emperor Constantine convened the Council at Hieria, he promised to name him patriarch if he would condemn icons and persuade the other bishops to do the same."

"So he changed his beliefs so he could become patriarch."

Elias's lips tightened. "It wasn't a real choice."

"What happened to him?"

"Two years ago, Emperor Constantine had the poor old man brought back to Constantinople and put through a diapompefsi. That means he was paraded naked through Constantinople sitting backwards on an ass so people could throw rocks and garbage at him. In the Hippodrome, Patriarch Nikitas the Slav, the new patriarch that Emperor Constantine had just appointed, read out his religious crimes, called anathemas. For each anathema, came a lash with a whip. Patriarch Nikitas the Slav sent the old man to his death without last rites. His body was thrown in the Cemetery of Pelagios outside the city walls, where they throw the bodies of criminals."

Chapter V

Our first glimpse of Hieria Palace was red tile roofs poking up behind white stone walls. A wide stone walkway connected it to a harbour where a warship rocked in the November wind. Elias squeezed us through the restless crowd until we were right by the warship. Sailors were climbing the masts and untying the white furled sails. Wind clattered the gangplank against the walkway. I could see the palace gates. Still closed.

"The Athens woman better come out soon," muttered a woman by me. "A storm is coming. I wouldn't trust those silk sails in a high wind."

"Not strong enough?" My eyes stayed on that closed gate.

"Our fishing boat sails under linen. I wouldn't risk anything lighter." She jerked her chin at a small fishing boat bobbing near the shore.

Elias began chatting with her but my eyes had caught a movement at the gate. They were swinging open! Twelve guards marched out. Their knee-length white tunicas with bright coloured panels down the front were belted with sashes the same red as their loose trousers. Curved swords crossed their backs. They stood at attention along both sides of the walkway and at the bottom of the bouncing gangplank.

A single slim figure stepped out. She stopped and looked from side to side like a curious child. How slim she was and how unafraid, even with all our eyes on her. Her plain green tunica stopped below her knees to show loose undyed linen trousers and linen shoes. A gold scarf bound her hair.

"Look at her all alone, poor little thing, and no fancy clothes, either," murmured the woman.

A young man stepped out behind her. His red tunica came to his knees, over white leggings. He said something. She moved forward, still looking from side to side. Then—and this I will never forget—she lifted her arms and waved. She turned all the way around, both arms waving with a smile on her like a girl having the time of her life. How beautiful she was, with that gold scarf flashing like the sun. People started calling out her name.

"Irini Athinea! Irini Athinea!" I heard my own voice join theirs.

The man spoke to her again. She looked at the gangplank heaving in the wind. She tossed a smile at us. Then, with a lift of her chin, she strode down the walkway. Ignoring the sailor's hand, she marched straight up the bucking ramp, then turned and raised both arms in triumph. Our happy shouts echoed off the palace walls.

She moved her hands to her throat. The golden scarf that bound her hair loosened. It floated upward into the white silk sails opening above her. Shining chestnut hair burst out like a storm cloud. She raised her arms. Flashes of white light bounced on those white silk sails that were slowly opening. Gasps slid through the crowd. Hands crossed hearts. I nudged Elias.

"She is catching the sunlight in the stones on her rings. We used to do that when we were children. Certain stones in our river have bits of sparkle. If we held them just right, we could dance light on the cottages."

At that moment, Irini opened her arms to us. It was an embrace, is what it was. She pulled us into her heart and held us there. I could feel it—everyone could. "Irini Athinea! Irini Athinea." A chant went up. It got louder and faster.

Precisely then, I swear, Irini of Athens looked straight at me. Our fates touched; I could feel it. She smiled, like the two of us shared a secret. She had the gift of making you think she saw you and only you. Later, I saw her do it often.

The sun slid behind dark clouds. The wind picked up. The warship eased out of the harbour. Only when the sails were fully open did she stop waving and go inside.

"That one knows how to please a crowd," muttered Elias. "Come on. We're getting in that fishing boat."

I stared in horror at the bobbing boat and the fisherman on shore holding it by a rope. The woman I had been chatting with was already in and beckoning to me.

"I can't swim!" I cried.

Elias picked me up and tossed me in like a sack of turnips. He and the fisherman vaulted in behind me. I clung to the side. Cold waves slapped my face. Salt spray stung my eyes. I fixed my eyes on the silk sails of the warship against the storm-darkening sky. I clutched Saint Thekla in the corner of my scarf. "Don't let us drown now that we're nearly there," I begged her.

Wind whipped us across the sea and soon we were right under the golden walls of Constantinople. Waves crashed against huge boulders at their base. The warship dropped its sails and slid into a harbour. Gates to other harbours were opening and letting other ships in. Elias was pointing and telling me something but I couldn't hear over the crashing waves and wind. We sailed past the end of the walls where they turned to go up a hill. There at the corner I saw three huge golden gates made of three golden arches. They were so tall and thick that the five golden elephants on top looked as small as wrens. The three gates were flanked by two enormous towers where two golden angels were poised to fly with their wings outspread. We shot past and pulled into a small harbour crowded with fishing boats.

"Rymin fishing village," Elias announced as the fisherman jumped out and hauled the boat onto the sand.

I crawled out on shaking legs and collapsed, gasping my thanks to Saint Thekla. When I had stopped shaking, I stumbled after Elias who was heading back towards those golden walls. As we neared, I saw that the walls were huge blocks of yellow stone with lines of red brick in between. Elias had said that one hundred thousand people lived in Constantinople. That November evening, I swear they were all trying to get in or out. A wooden bridge over a moat led to an open gate and into a vast courtyard. On the far side, rose the three arches of the Golden Gate.

That was when I saw Myrizikos. He was crossing the bridge. He was taller, wider across the shoulders, but he had the same smile. He was with some soldiers, all laughing as they came towards me. The ground tipped under my feet.

"Myri!" I screamed. "Myrizikos!"

He looked right at me. I know he saw me. Then he turned and ran up the road along the wall. The other soldiers ran with him. I chased him. People got in my way. I threw myself into one gap and then another, shouldering people aside, sobbing with joy that I had found him, and with fury that he was running away. I tangled with people coming out of a gate. I smashed into people coming out of another gate. At the third gate, I lost him.

"Did some soldiers come through here?" I panted at the guard.

"Why do you need them? I'm here for you, koukla mou," he leered.

I staggered over to a church opposite the gate and collapsed on the steps, sobbing and cursing Myrizikos with the last of my breath. After a while, I felt Elias sit down beside me.

"I saw him!" I sobbed. "He looked right at me. And then he ran the other way, the bastard!"

A big-bellied monk sprawled on the steps splashed water from a jug into a tin cup and brought it over. He put it in my hands.

"Holy water from at the Church of the Spring, which is just inside here, in the Monastery of the Life-Giving Spring, Zoodohos Pigi. Drink, kori mou. It will cure any sickness of body and soul." He watched me drink and refilled it for Elias.

I wiped my tears with my sleeve. "Did you see some soldiers go in that gate?"

"Soldiers are always coming and going out of that gate, kori mou. They drink the holy waters to cure what they get from the whores then they go back for more of what made them sick."

"Maybe he went in a gate that we passed," Elias suggested.

The monk nodded cheerfully. "Or he kept going. Up ahead there's the Gate of Rhesios by the Cemetery of Pelagios where they throw the bodies of criminals. Or there's the Fourth Military Gate or up Seventh Hill to the Gate of Saint Romanos by the church of that name."

"That's the last gate, Saint Romanos?" I was struggling to remember the names.

"One more, after you go downhill to the Lycus River that flows under the walls and up Sixth Hill, highest of the seven hills. There's more gates along the Golden Horn. That's a finger of the Propontis Sea."

The monk glanced at the sun nearly touching the sea. "City gates close at sunset. You need a bed for the night?" He glanced sideways at Elias.

"A convent."

"Ta Gastria Convent is closest. Go back where you came from and into Second Military Gate—between the two towers. Go past the public toilets and the amphi-theatre. When you get to Mesi Street, go left. Then right away take the steps down to the right. When you hear waves hitting the sea walls, look for a lamp in a niche by a gate. If it's lit, there's beds available. Best to hurry. It's a popular shelter."

We slipped through Second Military Gate as the sol-diers were swinging it closed. I used the public toilets, a rank wooden plank with holes suspended over a gutter. It was dark when I came out. I gripped the back of Elias's tunica.

"Myri saw me, I'm sure of it," I burst out. "Why did he run away?"

Elias muttered something that I didn't catch. We passed the shadowy tiers of what Elias said was an am-phitheatre and reached a street so wide that I thought it was a plateia. Men holding torches were climbing ladders and jamming them into the lamp poles. The ac-rid smoke made me cough. Tall buildings rose on both sides. People were sleeping in the entrances.

"Mesi Street," Elias said. "We go left, then down steps."

We stumbled down steps so dark I couldn't see my hand in front of my face. Finally, I heard the crash of waves. A candle flickering in a niche barely lit a shad-owy line of women moving through a gate. A nun was counting aloud.

"The lamp is still burning!" I exclaimed with relief and quickly joined the line. "Tomorrow morning, I'll start looking for Myrizikos at the place where I saw him."

Elias squeezed my arm. "Go left at the top of the lane

and Mesi Street will take you out the Golden Gate. May your saint guide your steps."

He was leaving! Shock took my breath. "Wait! Elias! Where are you going?" But my hand closed on air.

Two women bundled in long fur coats and fur hats pushed by me. The nun at the gate stopped the line and let them enter.

"Stinking rich paying guests," muttered a young woman behind me.

My purse held a few coins, but I didn't know if it was enough to pay for a bed. I decided to go ask the nun at the gate, but then I heard the thump of heavy footsteps on the steps and two armed soldiers bearing torches shoved us aside. They were guarding a slight figure in an ermine-hooded cloak.

"Spoilt Princess Anthusa," murmured the woman behind me. "Fourteen years old and wants to be a nun. The Emperor won't let her. So she comes here and pretends. She wears a hair shirt under her tunica, of all stupid-ass ideas. Empress Evdokia sponsors the convent so Abbess Pulkeria has to let Anthusa get what she wants. Which is her own room with a warm brazier and a wool mattress."

"Why would anyone give up being a princess to be a nun?" I asked, appalled.

The woman shrugged. "Empress Evdokia almost died having her. Maybe she wants to show her gratitude to God for letting her live." She drew her thin cloak closer around her throat. "What I wouldn't give for that ermine cloak. Move along or we won't get inside before the nun closes the gate."

"Do you come here often?" I edged forward.

"Whenever I need a good night's sleep. Abbess Pulkeria likes to think she is saving my soul. I'm Eleni. Where's your accent from?"

"I'm Thekla from Ikonion."

The line moved and we were in. In grateful relief, I inhaled the sweet aroma of vegetable stew. Light blazed from the long glass windows of a low building. I could see Princess Anthusa inside. A nun was lifting off her ermine cloak. Under it was a purple tunica.

"Under that is her hair shirt," snickered Eleni. "You can smell it when she walks by. Follow me and we'll get good beds. Then we line up for the latrine and wash basin, then into the church for Esperinos prayers. Then they feed us. Do you have a bowl and spoon?"

The dormitory was a large room jammed with narrow beds, as I could barely make out by the single oil lamp on a tall stand in the centre. Eleni tossed her bundle on a bed by the far wall.

"It's warmer away from the door. Your satchel is safe. One theft and Abbess Pulkeria throws everyone out."

The latrines were behind another building, A tallow candle lit five wooden seats over a trough. A novice was slinging buckets of water down the trough. A stone basin outside was for washing. I stumbled back to the courtyard and into the candlelit church where Eleni was huddled with other women for warmth, like sheep. I wrapped my fingers around Saint Thekla.

"Thank you for bringing me here," I whispered.

After prayers, we lined up in the dark courtyard and moved slowly into the kitchen. A tall thin nun was watching us from the doorway of the building where I had glimpsed Princess Anthusa. Her hands were folded across her waist, hidden under her sleeves.

"Abbess Pulkeria," murmured Eleni. "Mind your manners or she'll throw you out."

My stomach growled. I suddenly became aware of how cold and tired I was. "How I envy her," I sighed. "She has a roof over her head and a respected place in the world."

"She answers to Empress Evdokia. Not a fate to wish on anyone," muttered Eleni.

Inside the warm kitchen, I held out my wooden bowl and a novice ladled in thick vegetable stew from a steaming caldron. Another novice topped it with a hefty chunk of warm bread, and a third added a chunk of oxygala cheese. I followed Eleni into the refectory, a long room with a bare stone floor, two long tables and benches. We found two empty places near the end by a candle and stood holding our steaming bowls. I could see into a small side room. Three women were standing around a low table lit by a kandillia with six candles. They shone on thick cushions on a carpet and the glowing coals of a brazier.

"Princess Anthusa makes us wait so she can pray for our souls," muttered Eleni. "Ah, here she is. Her soul and ours are safe for the night."

Princess Anthusa's shadowy figure flicked along behind me. Other shadows followed her—a novice carrying her bowl and three novices bringing covered platters to the women dining in the side room. I saw Anthusa pause and glance into the side room. I imagined what stories the three rich women would tell when they got home. They had dined with the Emperor's daughter! But Princess Anthusa stood next to me.

"Put my bowl here," she ordered the novice. Her voice was high and demanding.

"Here?" The novice was startled.

"Here, I said!"

The novice set down the bowl on the table and hurried away. I caught the rank odour of stale sweat. The hair shirt. I fought the urge to laugh. Abbess Pulkeria entered and stood at the end of the table. By the feeble candlelight, I could see how thick and dark were her wool nun's tunica and the maforion that wrapped her hair, throat, and forehead. Black is expensive. It requires many dips in walnut dye. She slid her sharp eyes over our shadowed faces and smiled, the serene smile of a woman of God doing good work. She clasped her hands.

"Dear Lord, accept these poor lost sinners into Your bosom. Teach them gratitude for what they are about to receive. Amen."

Our Amens were drowned under the banging of shifted benches and the rattle of wooden spoons in wooden bowls. The stew was split pea, onion, and carrot, thickened with trahana. Delicious! The hefty oxygala cheese had the right sour tang and the barley bread was heavy and warm. This was a wealthy convent with many novices to labour over chores. I looked around for Abbess Pulkeria. She was eating with the rich guests.

Abruptly, Princess Anthusa stood up. "Have this. I don't want it." She pushed her bowl at me. She marched out the door.

The silence was so total that I could hear her boots

click across the courtyard. The nun at the door looked stunned. I started to reach for the bowl but Eleni grabbed my wrist.

"We eat what we are given, no more," she hissed.

The women started eating again. Eleni whispered between bites.

"Abbess Pulkeria would kick us out if we turned away our supper. She feeds us well without making us work for it. There's a hospice here too and the nursing nuns are kind. There's a school for little girls. But watch how you behave because if the Abbess doesn't like you, you never get back in."

I wiped my bowl clean with the last of my bread and followed Eleni to bed. Wrapped in my cloak with the wool blanket over me, I settled Saint Thekla in my hand and kissed her.

"We are in Constantinople!" I whispered. "Tomorrow we will find Myrizikos. We found him once, we'll find him again." I snuggled into the lumpy straw mattress. My thoughts wandered to Elias. I missed his warm body. He was probably climbing out of a hot bath and dressing for a big meal with his family in their big warm house. "Still, it feels good to be on our own again," I whispered to Saint Thekla, "Just you and me, like we started out."

Sometime later, women's soft voices woke me. The contemplative nuns who had chosen a life of prayer behind the wall of seclusion were chanting the prayers of the sixth hour after sunset. Not for me, that life. I went back to sleep.

Chapter VI

The claque of a wooden semantron woke me, the holy bell that Noah banged to welcome all creatures into the Ark. Half-asleep, I thought it was Father Damianos swinging the heavy log against the plank hanging by the church. Then I heard the clang of a bronze bell. It was time to rise and hurry down to the kapelarion in Amorion. Then came a clamour of church bells. Dorylaion? I opened my eyes.

Two novices were opening the dormitory double doors and letting in the damp grey dawn. Women were rising stiffly and folding their blankets. Shivering, I joined the line to the latrine, then splashed icy water from the basin on my hands and face. I was hungry and cold but my heart was light. Inside the church, I listened to the nuns chant the Orthros prayers. I slipped my fingers around Saint Thekla in the corner of my head scarf. "Myrizikos will be mine today!"

When I came out, the fog was gone. I gasped at the

brilliant flowers shining in the sun—purple cyclamen, yellow crocuses, and red anemones. Scarlet berries dotted the ivy cloaking the stone buildings. The trees in my village would be bright with autumn colour, I thought, attacked by homesickness. Then I remembered the sniggers that had chased me every time Myrizikos stood me up. I wasn't there to be laughed at now!

In the refectory, the fragrance of warm bread mingled with the stink of unwashed bodies. Princess Anthusa was still in the church. We waited, a roomful of poor women with rumbling stomachs watching our porridge cool. The Princess arrived, trailed by a novice bearing her bowl. Again she looked at the rich women. Again she ordered the novice to put her bowl by my place.

Abbess Pulkeria prayed for us to be grateful for our meal and went to eat with the rich women. I touched Saint Thekla tied in my head scarf and thanked her silently for bringing us here. I plunged my wooden spoon into my porridge.

"Raisins in the semolina! What a treat!" I said to Eleni next to me.

Princess Anthusa spoke without lifting her eyes from her bowl. "Our minds must stay on God and the saints while we eat. When I take my vows, I will eat with the nuns and be spared this disturbance."

Eleni rolled her eyes. I hid my smile.

Outside, I hoisted my satchel to my back, filled with purpose. I would go to the Golden Gate where I had seen Myrizikos and wait there until I found him. Elias had said to go up the steps to Mesi Street and turn left. But a novice hurried up to me as I was walking out the gate.

"Abbess Pulkeria wants you in her study."

Worried that I had broken some rule, I cautiously stepped through the open door of her study. And stopped, stunned by the glory before me. Sunlight through the tall glass windows flashed on shining many-armed silver kandilli. A table held gleaming silver plates and a green glass pitcher trimmed in gold with matching tiny glasses. Thick cushions sat on high-backed chairs. Oil lamps of blue glass banded in silver hung in the corners. Most wondrous were the thick pile rugs in bright floral designs.

A strange feeling came over me. I knew this room. I knew the rugs, the embroidered cushions, I even knew what lay inside that desk drawer. Saint Thekla, I thought to her. Are you sending me a memory of the future? Are you saying I am on the right path?

Abbess Pulkeria lifted her eyes from a table littered with wax tablets and papyrus sheets. She looked me over head to toe. "Take off your scarf. Turn around. Where is your birthplace?"

"A village near Ikonion in Anatolia, Abbess. My mother sent me here to work in my aunt's home." I folded my hands and lowered my eyes modestly.

"Don't lie," she snapped. "You are betrothed to a man who has deserted you. You are here searching for him."

I looked up, startled. She sighed, exasperated.

"Many young women like you find shelter here. Later, I see them begging in the street. And worse. Go home. A man who deserts a betrothal will desert a marriage."

I lifted my chin. "I have to find him, even if it is to end

the betrothal."

"Is he a soldier? Where is he billeted?"

"He's a guard in the Tagmata." Elias's warning came into my ears. I had to know his unit, Elias had said. I was on a fool's errand and the abbess knew it.

"How will feed yourself while you search?" she demanded.

"I will find work," I said stiffly. "I have experience. I took care of an old lady on my journey from Ikonion. I cooked and served table at a kapelarion in Amorion. I have a reference from the pandoheus and the pandokissa."

"Show me."

I dug the papyrus from my satchel and she took it over to the long window to read. She returned it to me and looked me over again. She nodded slowly as if making up her mind.

"A wealthy patroness of this convent wants a kitchen maid. She has a houseful of guests for the betrothal and wedding of Co-emperor Leon. The betrothal is tomorrow. Next week is the Feast of Saint Dimitrios and all the festivities around that. The wedding is the middle of December. You may be suitable. She will decide."

"Oh, thank you, Abbess." I felt dizzy. I had work!

"Patrikia Constanta is her name. She wants a peasant girl from a farm village. She believes they are healthier and more honest than city girls. This is not my experience, but it is not my place to argue. You will sleep here and have your morning and evening meals here. You will be paid. Half you will give to my ekonomis for your room and board."

"Thank you, Abbess." Paid work! And a safe bed. Saint Thekla was watching over me!

"Patrikia Constanta is an attendant to Empress Evdokia. Her husband is an anagrapheus in the Palace tax division. Patrikios Leon is his name. He maintains the tax registers. The title of Patrikios is granted only to very important people." The abbess savoured the words, proud of her connections.

"They have one daughter, Megalo. She is betrothed to a young favourite of the Emperor. His father was a governor of the Aegean Islands. He died and Emperor Constantine took over the boy's schooling. He will have a high position in the Palace. Empress Evdokia has appointed the boy's mother to be an attendant for the bride of Co-emperor Leon." Abbess Pulkeria folded her hands on the litter of papyrus. "I tell you this so you will understand that they are a wealthy and important family. Now listen carefully."

"I'm listening, Abbess."

"You will speak only to kitchen servants and only when you are spoken to. You will not repeat anything you overhear. The servants may say that Irini of Athens is too old to be a suitable bride, that she is an orphan and even more unsuitable. You may hear that Emperor Constantine brought her from Athens as an attendant for Princess Anthusa and changed his mind."

"I heard that she was to be an attendant to Empress Evdokia, Abbess."

"Do not repeat gossip!" she said sharply. "Empress Evdokia sponsors this convent. Princess Anthusa comes here to escape the banquets and parties that accompany this wedding, and the festivities surrounding the pagan Brumalia wine festival, no matter that the bishops condemn it." Abbess Pulkeria drew a breath to steady herself. "Whatever you see or hear, you will not repeat it here. Princess Anthusa has sharp ears. She will tell her mother."

"I will not gossip, Abbess."

"You will bathe and launder your clothing once a week. Excessive for a peasant, I know. However, wealthy families in Constantinople bathe even more. In summer they bathe daily. Go to the public baths near the Old Golden Gate on Mesi Street. If that garment you are wearing is all you have, the ekonomis will lend you a nun's habit."

"I have clean clothing, Abbess. In my village, we bathe and wash our clothes more than once a week," I added, stiffly.

"And lose your peasant accent so people can understand you."

"Yes, Abbess." I gave up pride of place and clothing.

"And eat properly. You gobble your food like a pig."

"Yes, Abbess." Did she have eyes in the back of her head? She had been eating with the rich women.

"You may be required to use a fork at your employment. Patrikia Constanta and Patrikios Leon use a fork at table. I have dined there and used one, myself." She preened herself, sliding her hand down the expensive grey wool of her nun's habit.

"Yes, Abbess." Fork? I didn't know what she was talking about.

Her gaze became stern. "Princess Anthusa spoke to

you."

"Yes, Abbess." She did have eyes in the back of her head.

"You may not speak to her, even if she addresses you. Princess Anthusa comes here to pray, not chat. She will take her vows when the Emperor allows. Some call him a godless barbarian who is the scourge of all God-loving monks and nuns who honour our saints. But he is the Hand of God on Earth, regardless of his drunken dancing during the Brumalia."

"Yes, Abbess."

"You may go." Her hands moved restlessly among the papyrus sheets littering her desk.

My relief at having work was now crashing against my need to find Myrizikos. How could I find him if I was stuck inside a kitchen? My eye fell on the mess of papyrus.

"I can read, Abbess. And write on wax tablets or papyrus. I did the accounts for my employer at the inn in Amorion. This was in my reference." I wondered how well she could read.

"Where did you gain this ability?"

"Our village priest taught us to read from the Rule of Saint Basil. And sums."

Abbess Pulkeria frowned at me suspiciously. She drew a wax tablet from her desk drawer. "Write these words of Saint Basil: 'He who sows courtesy reaps friendship.'" She handed me the tablet and a stylus and pointed to a table across the room.

I pulled out the stool and settled myself. I easily carved the words into the soft wax. I took it over to her. She was twitching the bits of papyrus around on her desk. She took the tablet to the window and held it to the light. She brought it back.

"Write the numbers one to twelve in a column, then add them up."

I did so. Then she told me to subtract the sum from one hundred. She glanced at my answer but not long enough to know if it was accurate. I wondered if she could do sums.

"The nun who manages our accounts is retiring to a convent in Bithynia. You may be able to take her place. We shall see how well you work for Patrikia Constanta. Do you have money for a bath?"

"Yes, Abbess."

She glanced out the long windows to the courtyard. Eleni was sitting on a bench rubbing something red onto her lips. Earrings sparkled at her ears.

"Tell Eleni to take you to the baths and then to the house of Patrikios Leon. She very likely knows the way." Her lips tightened.

"Thank you for trusting me, Abbess."

"I don't trust you. Or anyone. Only God." She began tidying the mess on her desk. She looked more cheerful.

Constantinople is a city of seven hills and that day I climbed four of them. I forgot the names of the statues and fountains that Eleni rattled off as we climbed up and down those steep hills. Men and women called out cheerful greetings to her. The women wore sparkling scarves around their throats and earrings and necklaces and shining bracelets. They looked like heteria, although much better dressed than my heteria friends in Amorion.

I didn't care who or what Eleni was, she was getting me started in this big city.

My eyes had not fooled me the night before about the width of Mesi Street. It was as wide as the plateia in my village where everyone gathered for festivals. It was also packed with people, oxen, mules, and slaves pulling carts and wagons up the steep cobblestone slope. On both sides were open platforms with pillars holding up the roofs.

"Colonnades," Eleni explained, exchanging happy greetings with vendors laying out wares. "At the back are passageways called stoa. More shops are inside the stoa."

The usual water troughs carrying filth ran down both sides of Mesi street. I pulled my scarf over my mouth and nose.

"It stinks worse in summer," said Eleni, cheerfully. "Here we are, the Old Golden Gate baths."

The warm wet room was noisy with the chatter of naked women getting washed by fleshy hairless eunuchs. Eleni was well known. Quickly she and the eunuchs got my story.

"If Myrizikos is a guard in the imperial Tagmata, you'll find him," everyone agreed.

"Or you'll decide that a man who runs away isn't worth chasing," Eleni added.

My clothes I left to be laundered. Nothing could be done about the holes in my boots. Now that I had work, I could buy new ones. Back on Mesi Street, I gawked at the tall buildings of wood or brick on Seventh Hill. Some were five stories high. People were leaning out windows calling to friends below. Laundry lines zigzagged across side lanes so narrow that I could touch the buildings on both sides. We entered an archway into a round plateia surrounded by colonnades. People were filling jugs from a splashing fountain. Vendors were spreading out their wares and shouting out prices. We stopped for a rest on the steps of a wide stone roofed porch that Eleni called a portico. There was a tall pillar in the centre. A shabby man was sitting on top.

"He's a stylite monk. They can sit up there for months," said Eleni. "They drop down a basket and people put food in it. You can imagine the filth down below."

We went on and my eyes I searched for Myrizikos. But he was nowhere to be found. Mesi Street dropped down steeply and we walked through an archway into another forum surrounded by porticos and colonnades.

"Forum of the Ox," Eleni said. "Right here, I saw the monk Andrew of Crete get executed with an axe for praising icons. That same year the Emperor made the army vow not to pray before them. Some soldiers I know didn't want to swear because they like having a painting of their saint on the inside of their shields for protection. But they adore the Emperor and they took the oath like the rest." She waved at a soldier who blew her kisses. I pulled my scarf over my mouth and nose.

The shops got nicer after the Forum of the Ox. Stone slabs covered the filth in the gutters as we climbed Third Hill. We passed through a wide plateia paved with marble.

"This is the Philadelphion, the centre of Constantinople," Eleni said. "Mesi Street divides here. One leg goes up Fourth Hill to the Church of Holy Apostles. All our emperors are buried there."

Mesi Street was so crowded now that servants were walking in front of their masters shouting, "Clear the way!" We passed under a tall marble arch topped by two bronze statues of women, into a large oval forum with a marble column in the centre so tall that the statue on top looked like a child's toy.

"That's Constantine the Great up there and this is the Forum of Constantine. Everyone passes through here. For the Brumalia wine festival, the Emperor sends huge cheese wheels and hams here. And dancers and jugglers and magicians and music. Lots of fun and good for my business. That red building with the gold dome and the red pillars is the Senate House. The big naked statue is Zeus. The bronze statue over there is Athena. The old gods. The building over there with the bronze doors is the Library."

Eleni waved at some soldiers lounging at the base of the column. She looked at me earnestly. "You've done well, Thekla of Ikonion, getting work and a place to sleep. But if you ever get in trouble, come to these steps. I'll be here or my friends will find me."

Her kindness brought tears to my eyes.

Mesi Street from The Forum of Constantine to the Great Palace is called the Imperial Road, I learned as we walked along it. At the end stood a low building made of four pillars and a curved roof.

"The Milion. Where all roads in the empire begin," Eleni said.

I stared at it. I had reached the end of my journey.

And the beginning of my new life. Eleni pulled me to a small eatery.

"Let's have a bite to eat. Soon you'll be worked off your feet and so will I."

Eleni pulled out her bowl and a vendor ladled out chickpea and carrot stew. I bought a roasted sausage wrapped in warm flatbread and we ate it sitting on the steps of the Milion. The spicy taste of fennel seed filled my mouth. Hot fat dripped off my chin. Eleni pointed at some massive bronze gates topped by a curved arch. On it pranced four life-sized bronze horses.

"The Hippodrome," Eleni mumbled. "Chariot races. Also where the army brings the prisoners. I saw old Patriarch Constantine brought through here sitting backwards on a donkey, naked. They beat him and dragged him away and cut off his head."

I shuddered and turned my eyes to the rivers of people. No Myrizikos. Eleni pointed at a gate in the stone wall behind the Milion.

"Inside there is a big open area called the Augustaion. The Church of Holy Wisdom is in there. So is the entrance to the Great Palace, Chalke Gate. The barracks for the Tagmata are just inside Chalke Gate. Let's go ask the guards if they have heard of your Myrizikos."

Suddenly my legs went clumsy and heavy. I felt sick. I followed Eleni through the gate and across a huge plateia paved in white marble. We walked over to a square structure set against the Palace wall made of four pillars and a rounded roof. Some guards whistled at us and shouted rude remarks.

Eleni smiled at them. "Hey boys, we're looking for a

Myrizikos of Ikonion. Any of you seen him?"

"Never heard of him. Why do you need him? You have us!"

Disappointment felt bitter in my mouth and my eyes filled with tears. I pulled my head scarf across my face and turned away. Eleni took my arm.

"Never mind those pigs. I'll ask around. I know a lot of soldiers. Now forget your home town soldier. You've got a long day's work ahead of you."

Chapter VII

Patrikia Constanta and Patrikios Leon lived on a narrow lane behind the Church of Holy Wisdom. The wooden two-story red house had a balcony that jutted over the street. Eleni hammered on a small door next to an iron-studded carriage gate. A tall bald eunuch in a long white tunica listened coldly to my stammered explanation and let me in.

I barely heard Eleni's cheerful farewell, I was gaping like the village idiot. The courtyard was paved in flat green stones. Balconies dripped with vines. Most wondrous was the glittering fountain that splashed into a pool. The bottom sparkled with bits of coloured glass shaped into flowers. It was even more grand than the fountain at Auntie Sofia's in Nicaea. The eunuch led me down steps into a long kitchen. Shelves shone with green glass goblets and jugs, bright ceramic serving bowls and coloured plates. At the end of the kitchen was a hearth where a huge pot hung on a bar over a fire. A wide door opened to a courtyard where fires burned under two stoves covered by a roof. Smoke was billowing.

A heavy bald man, probably a eunuch, was rolling out dough on a slab of marble. A plump woman was chopping leeks and carrots on a wooden table and tossing them into a pot. A girl in a short tunica and bare legs was scrubbing laundry in a deep sink. Water drained through a hole under the window into the side yard.

The tall eunuch announced me. "Thekla from Ikonion in Anatolia. Abbess Pulkeria sent her." He pointed at the fat man. "Cook Akepsimas will decide if you stay."

The thick man looked me over without slowing his rolling pin. "Patrikia Constanta asks for kitchen help and we get a peasant wearing what she slept in. Can they speak proper Greek in Anatolia or do we need a translator?" He pointed a thick finger at a pile of fish on a table. "Gut those. You won't have to talk for that."

The plump woman put down her knife and found me an apron. "I'm Aspasia. Take no notice of Akepsimas," she said, giving the cook a reproving look. "He's cranky because Patrikia Constanta just told him she wants fowl baked in pastry tonight instead of roast venison like we had planned. You're sorely needed. We've got eight for mid-day meal. Fish soup."

She handed me a small sharp knife and pointed at the fish. "This is sea bass, that's flounder, this is carp. The little ones are red mullet. I bought them off the fishing boat at Psamatia Harbour this morning. We serve the red mullet on the side. The rest go in the soup. Can you clean fish?"

"River trout. What's in the bucket?" I stared doubtfully

into stinking dark water.

"Shrimp, mussels, scallops. Gut the fish then I'll show you how to clean those. Fish heads, fins, and tails go in my pot with the leeks for broth. Guts go in that pot for garum. Scrape off the scales and put the fish on that platter. We'll boil them in the broth. You know."

I didn't. We never served fish soup at Amorion. But fish are fish, I discovered when I stuck the point of the knife in the shit hole and slit open the belly. As they piled up on the platter, my confidence grew. I tossed the heads, fins, and tails into Aspasia's pot, she added parsley, bay leaf and thyme, and together we moved the heavy vessel to the stove. She filled a pitcher with water from a tap on the wall, poured it in and added a splash of clear wine.

On to the mussels. Aspasia showed me how to trim the fur off the shell. I nicked my finger first thing and it stung every time I put my hand in the bucket. I had the pile half done when Akepsimas shouted at me to bring him one. He looked at it like it was pig turd.

"Wrong. All wrong. Bring me that knife and I'll show you how to do it right."

My back ached and my arms itched from the guts and scales. I would have to scrub down at the public baths before I went back to the convent. The laundry maid snickered. Anger surged. I picked up the knife and glanced at the eunuch to gauge the distance. I would pin his tunica to the chopping block, right at his groin. I raised my arm.

"This knife, Akepsimas?" I smiled sweetly.

His face went pale. A hand came behind me and

slipped over the knife handle. Aspasia murmured in my ear. "Don't get yourself in trouble the first day."

Akepsimas resumed rolling out dough. "Aspasia, you show her," he muttered hoarsely.

Getting their shells off the shrimp wasn't as hard as cleaning the scallops. Aspasia had the broth simmering by then.

"Fish soup is made of fish, shellfish, and vegetables in a broth. We boil the fish whole in the broth. When they're done, we take them out, bone them, and put them back with the shellfish. All of it goes into a tureen with a little fresh ginger scraped over the top. The House Manager upstairs ladles out the bowls at the table. He adds a raw quail's egg and a ball of soft goat cheese to each."

The upstairs servants came down then and we sat around the work table to eat before we started feeding the family and guests.

"Leftovers," shrugged Aspasia, pulling me down beside her.

But what leftovers! Slices of cured loin of pork steeped in vinegar and rubbed with honey and black pepper. Spicy smoked sausages that Aspasia explained had been cooked with kitron and pepper and cumin and bayberry. There were pickled beets and vinegar cucumbers with garlic. This family ate well! Table gossip was all about Irini of Athens.

"Empress Evdokia has appointed Megalo to be a 'Friend' of Irini of Athens," explained the House Manager, the eunuch who had opened the door to me. "'Friend' is an actual Palace position. They are supposed to teach her what to say, how to dress, explain her official duties, that sort of thing. There are two other 'Friends'. They don't get paid, like Patrikia Constanta does for being an attendant. Empress Evdokia told the Athens woman that there is no money in the budget for attendants."

"The other two will have do the teaching," sniffed the upstairs maid. "Megalo can't even dress herself and she's already nine years old."

"How did Megalo get chosen?" I asked.

The House Manager explained. "Irini of Athens told Empress Evdokia that she wanted someone younger than the other 'Friends'. Patrikia Constanta suggested Megalo." He snickered. "Nine years old. That will teach Irini of Athens to complain."

"Who are the others?" asked Aspasia.

"Doti, the mother of the lad who is betrothed to Megalo. He is called Fanis," he added for my benefit. "Also nine years old. They will wed when they are fourteen. The third Friend is called Tisti. Married to some Palace administrator. They often come here with their son, Theodore."

Later, I was to know these women well. But then, all I could manage was to keep up with the talk about the banquet that Patrikia Constanta were planning for Co-emperor Leon and Irini of Athens.

"Fourteenth of November," announced the House Manager. "The last fast day until after Nativity. Twenty-five guests."

"Where will they all sit?" demanded Aspasia, crossly, which set off grumbling about the amount of cooking for the many houseguests, the extra laundry and piss pots that had to be emptied into the latrine in the courtyard that was filling up with all the piss pots. Then we started putting the appetizers together. There were three kinds of olives plus sturgeon eggs and capers with oil and vinegar poured over them. Also four different cheeses. Aspasia slipped me a taste and I made a face; not nice like our village goat cheese. The upstairs servants took it upstairs and we got the fish broth strained and the fish and shellfish cooked in the broth. We poured it into a tureen and put the red mullet on a warmed platter.

The upstairs servants brought down the appetizer plates. The fish broth went up with the House Manager and Akepsimas carried the platter of mullet followed by two servants with the warmed bowls. It was like in Amorion when four coaches came in at once and I was hustling platters as fast as cook could slap the meat on them.

We had a bit of a sit-down and drank some mountain tea and ate the appetizers that they didn't finish upstairs. Then I was scrubbing plates and Akepsimas was sending up the sweet which was quince soaked in sweet wine and sprinkled with kinammomon, topped with soft white cheese. Aspasia slipped me a taste. Delicious!

I was set to plucking a chicken and a partridge for the pastry dish that evening. Akepsimas hacked them into chunks and dropped them into a pot simmering on the outdoor stove. Aspasia was peeling carrots and parsnips and putting them in to boil while I stirred sesame seeds into honey to be mashed into the boiled vegetables. What a confusion of delicious smells! In Amorion, all I ever smelled was smoke.

By then, it was nearing dusk. Akepsimas told me I could leave. "Be here early tomorrow," he growled without looking at me. I gave him a big smile. Saint Thekla had found me work!

Aspasia walked with me, otherwise I would have been lost ten times over. The Imperial Road was ablaze with torches, not like Amorion where it went dark when the sun went down. Even Nicaea and Nikomidia had night torches only in the big plateias. Here, people were chatting on the colonnades or leaning out windows and talking to people below. I heard drums and trumpets. Aspasia sighed with resignation.

"Emperor Constantine and his family are coming back from the Church of Holy Apostles. They pray there two or three times a week. Mesi Street will be blocked for ages. Let's go by the back lanes."

But I wanted to see the procession, so she agreeably got us places up on a colonnade with a good view. The imperial guards were first. I searched each face for Myrizikos. My breath caught over and over when I thought I saw a familiar slant of shoulder or the way a soldier turned his head. Then all thought of Myrizikos vanished. Emperor Constantine rode up to the Milion on his white horse and turned it around to face us. He was so near, I could see the band of shining gold on his head. His long fair hair was tied back with a leather thong, his beard was trimmed close to his face, and his wide moustaches shone with wax. His glittering silver tunica was slit up the front and back so that it lay flat over his legs. A short purple cape covered one shoulder. He raised his hand.

It was a blessing. And a vow. My heart felt the power. He was telling us that he stood between us and the barbarians at our borders. We were why he was born, he was saying—this violent man who conscripted my brothers and forced us to sell our sheep to the army at below market prices, and taxed every bushel of barley we coaxed from the earth. I dropped flat in full obeisance like everyone around me. With all my heart I asked God and the saints to keep our powerful emperor safe.

Emperor Constantine reined his white horse around and rode into the Augustaion. I climbed to my feet, shaken by a force that I could not name. Aspasia shook my arm and pointed.

"Look! Irini of Athens! God in Heaven, she's beautiful!" She went quiet. So did everyone around us. I could scarcely breathe.

She was the most beautiful woman I had ever seen. At Hieria Palace, she had been lovely and charming but still a young girl in all innocence waving at a crowd. Now she was an elegant woman sitting easily astride a brown mare, smiling from side to side. Her cheeks were flushed and her dark eyes were enormous. She had pushed her blue scarf off her hair and her masses of chestnut hair were held back with jewelled clips.

Co-emperor Leon rode next to her on a grey gelding. He had his father's fair hair but his moustache was straggly and his beard was a joke. He had narrow shoulders and a pinched face and uneasy eyes that flicked nervously from side to side.

"Can't pull a hair from a thin beard," Aspasia muttered the old saying. Someone sniggered. I wondered what Irini of Athens had thought when she walked down the gangplank and found this specimen at the bottom. Whatever she thought then, now she looked deliriously happy.

The colonnade was high enough so I was eye-to-eye with the riders. As she passed, she turned her head and looked at me. I swear she recognized me. She dipped her hand into the purse at her waist and flung a coin high into the air but straight at me. My quick peasant fingers captured it. A silver milaresion! A beggar nearly got it but my knife pricked his throat and the silver disc stayed in my hand.

Aspasia was pointing. "That's the Emperor's oldest son from Empress Evdokia, Kaisar Christoforos. Next to him is Kaisar Nikiforos. They are fourteen and eleven. The little one on the pony is Prince Nikitas. He's six. Prince Evdokimos is with Princess Anthusa in the carriage. She's the twin sister of Kaisar Christoforos. The three old ladies beside her are Emperor Constantine's sisters. Empress Evdokia isn't here because she's still isolated after the birth of Anthimos."

We left, caring nothing for the scarlet-robed priests shuffling in their tall red mitres. Just as I was climbing down the steps from the colonnade, I caught sight of a familiar figure. He was on a horse in the midst of obviously wealthy men behind the priests.

"Elias!" I blurted. I gaped at his rich velvet cloak fastened at the neck with a glittering jewelled brooch and his long red tunica split over green trousers. I stepped back to hide in the crowd as his quick eyes searched for whoever had called his name. My worn cloak was frayed at the bottom and I stank of fish. I knew Elias wasn't a monk but I had no idea he came from such wealth. I blushed, remembering how I had called this rich man a liar, and how I had slept in his arms.

Aspasia lived near the wide open area paved in marble that Eleni had called the Philadelphion. We stopped at a narrow alley. "I moved in with my two sisters when my husband died. My sons and their families live in the apartment below. They own a stall in the clothing market. My husband was in the carpenter's guild so I get a small pension. I saw you staring at the Emperor's guards. Are you looking for a certain soldier, koritzaki mou?"

I was too tired to lie. Seeing how wealthy Elias was had made me feel small and hopeless. We sat down on the base of a statue of three men and I talked. Aspasia put her arm around me.

"Find another man, Sweetie. If this one left you once, he'll leave you again."

"I have to get him to release me from my betrothal vow," I said, miserably. As I walked down Mesi Street, I held Saint Thekla in my hand. "We must take heart, Saint Thekla," I said to her. "We haven't found Myrizikos but I have work and safe lodgings. And two friends. I will save my earnings. When Myrizikos and I are wed, we will live in a big apartment near Aspasia."

The street torches came farther apart after the Philadelphion. I tightened my shawl around my throat and pulled the hood of my cloak farther over my head. I hid my face under my scarf. Finally my anxious eyes spotted the broken arch of the Old Golden Gate and after that, I turned down the dark steps to the wavering candle in the niche and the line of poor women hoping for a meal and a bed. I went to the head of the line—not a rich woman but a paying boarder with a guaranteed bed. I was no longer a poor woman without a home.

I could barely keep my eyes open through our supper of cracked wheat soup thick with cabbage and bitter greens. "Life is different for the rich," I whispered to Saint Thekla as I fell asleep in the crowded dormitory listening to the tramp of the night watchman.

Dense morning fog filled the courtyard when the bang of the semantron woke me at dawn. I walked up Mesi Street with the other boarders at Ta Gastra who were also working in wealthy homes. The statues atop the colonnades in the Forum of the Ox wavered in the fog. Was that the headless ghost of Andrew the monk? We pulled our cloaks tight around us. The bronze weathervane woman on Third Hill creaked in the wind and the wet crept into the holes in my boots. But at the Forum of Constantine, a weak sun was polishing the gold statue of the Great Constantine and soldiers were throwing back the hoods of their leather coats.

Akepsimas assigned me to make the breakfast millet porridge and ladle it into bowls set on trays. Aspasia coached me and I managed to do it without burning it. The upstairs servants took them to the bedchambers. But with so many guests, there were a lot of breakfast trays to take up. So the following morning, Aspasia thrust a tray into my hands.

"This goes to Megalo. Top of the stairs. Stir up her brazier and wake her up. I'll show you the way." She picked up another tray.

We crossed a long central room where a servant was

stirring up glowing coals in a brazier. Thick pile carpets covered the floor. Heavy cushions lined the walls. Here the family met, ate, and received visitors. A polished sideboard held a shelf of scrolls and codices. I peered at bits of broken coloured glass and small pottery figures the size of my palm.

"Roman glass from ship wrecks and other old stuff that Patrikios Leon collects," whispered Aspasia.

Megalo's bedchamber was cold. I set the tray on a table and stirred the embers in the brazier and added a few coals. A small voice came from under the quilts.

"Bring my tray over here. What is it?"

"White bread warm from the bakery, plum and raisin compote, fresh goat milk from the man with his donkey, millet porridge with honey."

"Take away the icky porridge and the slimy compote."

"Can I eat it?"

She giggled and sat up. She was small, with a child's round face and tousled dark hair. I set the tray on her lap and sat on the end of her bed to eat the compote with her silver spoon. I hadn't had fruit since Auntie Sofia's villa in Nicaea. I polished off the porridge, too. Megalo giggled as I sucked the honey off the spoon. She nibbled on the bread and yawned. Clothing was strewn about the room. I started to fold it and caught sight of myself in a tall, polished silver mirror fixed to the wall. I had only ever seen my face. Was this me? This tall woman with thick dark hair and long legs and narrow waist? Was this what Elias had seen?

"Paint your lips and put on earrings and men won't take their eyes off you," came Megalo's shy little voice.

"I don't know about that," I shrugged. I glanced at some necklaces and earrings and bracelets jumbled on the table. "You should look after your nice jewellery."

"It's my mother's. She makes me wear it at the Palace. I'm a Friend for Irini of Athens. Me and two boring old ladies. We're supposed to teach Irini how to behave like a princess, now that she's actually betrothed. She never does what we tell her. Really, we're spies for Empress Evdokia. But I don't spy."

"Why not?"

"Doti and Tisti tell the empress, first."

"What is she like, Irini of Athens?" She had hovered in my thoughts ever since Hieria.

She yawned. "People snigger at her funny accent. She was on a warship for a month with Emperor Constantine. God only knows what happened there, my mother says. Doti and Tisti pray for her soul. She told them her soul is doing very well without their prayers. Tisti has five children. She won't let her husband come to her bed anymore. She wants to be a nun."

"Why doesn't she take the vows and go to a convent?" I drank the warm goat milk.

"And give up her rich house and servants? She has a terrible temper. She beats her servants then she makes them kneel with her to pray for forgiveness. That's what Doti said."

She snuggled into the quilts. "Irini made me go with her to the theatre last night. Doti and Tisti refused. They said the play was pagan and would corrupt their souls. I fell asleep. Afterwards, Irini wanted grilled shrimp so her eunuch took us to a dirty kapelarion by the Hippodrome. I wouldn't eat anything. I'm going back to sleep. Irini won't get up 'til noon."

When I brought down the empty tray, Aspasia gave me a sideways look. "Megalo usually only eats the bread. I let the porridge harden and fry it for our lunch."

The Feast of Saint Dimitrios a few weeks later brought even more houseguests. Aspasia had to shop twice a day and Akepsimas sent me with her to help carry. My heart lifted! I could search for Myrizikos! And I did, those first days. Every soldier drew my eye. But soon Irini of Athens took my gaze. We often saw her in the markets with Megalo and her two other Friends. There were two boys with them too.

"They are Doti's son, Fanis, and Tisti's son, Theodore," Megalo told me later. "Irini's cousin is always with her, too. She calls him Theo, short for Theophylaktos. He came with her from Athens." I remembered seeing him getting on the warship with her at Hieria Palace.

Aspasia and I saw them leaving Sampson Hospital when we were shopping in the big market behind the Church of Holy Wisdom. Doctors were bowing to them. Out of curiosity, we followed them into the Church of Saint Irini by the hospital, then to the Forum of Leon nearby where Irini tossed coins to poor children. Another day, we saw them coming out of the Library. Servants were carrying scrolls and codices. Once when we were in the meat market, we were near enough hear Irini of Athens ask the price of donkey meat. I liked her Athens accent.

Aspasia was teaching me how to shop and bargain well. "I buy donkey meat from Cremona only, and gazelle from Anatolia. And ox and buffalo freshly slaughtered," she said. We bought pork at the hiremporia and lamb and mutton at the makelarion. "Best is one-year-old castrated males," she told me.

"Female goat tastes better than male." I wanted to show I knew something.

I saw Irini of Athens and her group in the artopios where I went twice a day for bread. Patrikia Constanta liked white wheat bread that was yeast-raised and salted. I bought it glazed with almond oil or with spices kneaded in, like anise or fennel seed or mastic. She especially liked it decorated with linseed, sesame, or poppy seeds. We servants ate coarse barley bread, of course.

One day, Aspasia and I saw Irini and her group in the Jewish quarter coming out of the Church of the Mother of God of the Copper Market. We were returning from Psamatia Harbour where the fish was cheaper sold off the fishing boats than at the ikthyopratia in the main market.

"She's praying before the belt of the Mother of God to get herself with child," Aspasia said. "The priest will drape it around her and she will become with child."

Constantinople became my village. I learned its markets, streets, and alleyways—a feast for my eyes and my memory. Eagerly, I stored up my wisdom for when I would marry Myrizikos and live near Aspasia in a big apartment off Mesi Street.

Princess Anthusa came often to Ta Gastria, cutting in front of the line and making us wait while she prayed in the church. She always sat by me. I could smell her stinking hair shirt. One evening, snow began falling as I walked back to the convent. The heavy wet flakes quieted the great city, like in my village when even the sheep stop their mutterings in the face of nature. Snow whitened the shoulders of the poor women waiting to enter the convent. A shadow stepped out as I passed the narrow passage leading to the guest rooms. Startled, I slipped and nearly fell.

"Follow me." Princess Anthusa turned towards her room.

"Abbess Pulkeria forbade me to speak to you," I stammered.

"Do as I say!" She moved into the passage, her footsteps silent in the snow.

I pulled up my hood to hide my face from the Abbess who was standing in her doorway as usual, keeping an eye on the women filing through the gate.

The guest rooms were in a low building around a small courtyard. Oil lamps burned in niches by each door. God forbid the rich should carry their own lamps. Princess Anthusa opened her door. Light spilled out. She had left an oil lamp burning on the bedside table beside a prayer rope, a shocking waste of oil. The room was warmed by a glowing brazier. Thick rugs covered the floor. There was even a commode. The rich cannot toilet with the poor. Princess Anthusa held out her hand.

"Give me your icon."

Shocked, I didn't move. I couldn't believe my ears.

"The icon you conceal in your scarf," she snapped impatiently. "Don't deny it. Your hand moves there often. It isn't your purse; that is on a strap around your neck. It has to be an icon. Who is the saint? Answer me!

Tell me the name, I command you!"

"Saint Thekla of Ikonion, First Woman Martyr and Equal to the Apostles. She is my name saint."

She sat abruptly on the bed and clenched her small hands. "I don't have a name saint. I am named after an abbess who predicted my birth. Why do you touch your icon?"

I answered cautiously. "To feel safe. To know she is safe."

Her voice was choked. "I have never even seen an icon. I know the monks paint them; my father burns their monasteries because of it. I long to hold one between my hands, to feel the presence of a saint." She put a hand across her eyes. "I cannot bear the Palace any longer. I sit at banquets where people eat excessively and gossip about each other. That harlot from Athens speaks to me and I must answer. Her parentage is unknown. She chews with her mouth open and licks her fingers like a barbarian. She says that a fork is a trident given to us by the god Poseidon. My mother says that she knew Father improperly on his warship. My mother will break the engagement and send her back to Athens. Or to that prison convent on Lesbos where she will die." She held out her hand. "Give me your icon."

Anger flushed out my shock. "No. You will keep her. You will tell Abbess Pulkeria and she will throw me out."

"Give her to me or I will have you executed."

"Then you will burn in hell fires like the Romans who martyred Saint Thekla."

A sob wrenched from her. "I won't tell Abbess Pulkeria. I promise. Please, I beg you, let me hold your icon just for a moment. I will give her back. My life is a misery. Give me the comfort that she gives you."

My heart twisted. Slowly I untied the knot in my scarf and held out Saint Thekla.

Chapter VIII

I was so shaken by Princess Anthusa touching Saint Thekla that I slipped on the ice outside the guest rooms and dropped her in the snow. Breathless with panic, I crawled around scrabbling until the tiny bit of wood came into my numb fingers. I rubbed off the snow and Princess Anthusa's greedy touch and knotted the saint back in my head scarf. Then I joined the line of women creeping toward the kitchen. I barely tasted the lentil soup. In bed, I lay rigid, clasping Saint Thekla over my heart.

"We will find a new home tomorrow," I whispered. "We aren't safe here anymore."

The next day was Saturday and payday at the house of Patrikios Leon. I could not join the usual light-hearted banter as we stepped forward to accept our wages from the House Manager. My feet dragged as Aspasia and I walked home down Mesi Street. What if Princess Anthusa again demanded to have Saint Thekla? What if imperial guards were waiting at the convent to take me to prison and cut off my ears and my tongue?

"Tomorrow is Sunday. We work a half day," Aspasia reminded me. "I'll take you to the other barracks in the city. If we don't find your Myrizikos, we can walk up the road along the land walls and ask at the city gates. Maybe you'll decide to give up this search and find a better man."

We agreed to meet at the Philadelphion. I would also look for another convent to live, I decided. I was respectfully employed, I had money to pay for room and board. Hope lifted my heart. It crashed when I got to the gate of Ta Gastria.

"Abbess Pulkeria wants you in her study," the nun told me.

The abbess locked the door behind me and pulled the drapes over the long windows to the courtyard. She held out her hand. "Give me your icon."

"Princess Anthusa promised she would not tell you. She lied," I said, defiantly.

Abbess Pulkeria tightened her lips. "She is a princess. She can do whatever she wants. You cannot. Your icon is a danger to this convent. And to the home of Patrikia Constanta."

"Princess Anthusa wants my icon. She will make you give it to her."

The abbess sat down on her chair as if her legs had given out. She put her face in her hands. "She threatened to tell the Emperor that I am harbouring icons. He will revoke our charter and throw us all in the street. He did it to the Akimeti monks at Studios Monastery. I saw the soldiers whipping them out the Golden Gate."

"Do not believe her threats," I said urgently. "Princess Anthusa will not tell the Emperor. He will have my icon burnt and she wants it. She won't let that happen."

Abbess Pulkeria wrung her hands. "Think, child. If Princess Anthusa saw your icon, so will others. The poor women here—even my nuns—could see it and confess to the priest. He will inform the bishop and we are finished."

"Saint Thekla will not let this happen."

The abbess sighed. "Saint Thekla is your icon? I used to carry the icon of my name saint tied in my scarf. When I came here as a novice, I had to give her up. Consider the danger you put us in, my child. Emperor Constantine locked hundreds of bishops inside Hieria Palace until they banned icons. He threw the precious relic of Saint Euphemia into the sea because people were kneeling before it. Mihalis the Dragon has dragged monks and nuns from their monasteries. He made them hold hands while people spit on them. I witnessed the monk Andrew being dragged through these streets until he died. Give me your icon, child. Keep all of us safe."

"I cannot live without Saint Thekla. She guides my steps."

"Then you must leave this convent."

"I will find another place to live." I turned to the door.

"Wait!" She threw up her hands. "Don't leave. Patrikia Constanta is happy with you. Megalo gets up on time. She even eats her porridge. If Patrikia Constanta discovers you have left, she will want to know why. She will stop her donations. Worse, Princess Anthusa will tell Empress Evdokia. The empress will tell the Emperor to revoke our charter. I will keep your icon safe. I will return her when you leave. Perhaps the day will come when another emperor will allow us our icons."

I shook my head. "You will give her to Princess Anthusa. She has never known hunger, never had holes in her boots. She gets whatever she wants. She will get my saint."

"She will not have her. I promise. You will have your saint back when you leave."

With stiff fingers, I freed Saint Thekla from my scarf and placed her upon the outstretched hand of Abbess Pulkeria. Saint Thekla vanished into her pocket. My legs could barely hold me. I collapsed onto a snowy bench in the courtyard, my heart an empty hole in my breast. I had betrayed my beloved saint. She had kept me from the Valley of Death when the old granny died. She had guarded me when I slept with Elias in haylofts and forests. She had led me to Ta Gastria. And I had sent her into the greedy hands of Princess Anthusa.

Besides that failure, I hadn't found Myrizikos. Despair flooded me. Then came a hot blast of anger. I could take revenge on Anthusa and Abbess Pulkeria. I only had to find a priest. I would tell him that Abbess Pulkeria had an icon.

***

A certain quiet settles over Constantinople on Sunday. Shops and workshops are closed by law and just a few eateries are open. Only church bells break the blessed silence. Aspasia and I climbed the snowy hills of Constantinople asking the guards at the various army barracks for Myrizikos. They laughed and made lewd remarks. Angry and frustrated, Aspasia and I went out the Golden Gate to ask at the gates in the land walls.

The three arches of the Golden Gate are for imperial processions. We passed through the smaller gate beside it, and crossed the courtyard under the gaze of the golden angels. Outside the walls, we turned up the road where I had chased Myrizikos. The soldiers at all the gates delivered only rude invitations. We gave up at dusk. Wearily, I returned to the convent. Eleni was standing in line to get in.

"Been out looking for your soldier?" she commented.

I was tired, discouraged, cold, and hungry. "I've searched everywhere. I don't know where else to look."

"Abbess Pulkeria got your icon off you, didn't she?" she murmured with a sympathetic glance.

I was shocked. "You knew I had an icon?"

"I slept next to you, didn't I? I saw you take something in your hand and kiss it."

She squeezed my arm. "Don't worry. The abbess takes them off all the village girls. She gives them back when they leave."

"She won't give mine back. She will give her to Princess Anthusa," I said bitterly. I told her the story. "I don't want to live here anymore. Can I stay with you?"

She laughed and shook her head. "No, Sweetie. You are not suited for my life. Maybe some servant at Patrikia Constanta's house needs a paying boarder."

No one did. Even Aspasia didn't have room. Elias would know a place I could stay, I thought. His rich family might have space in their servant quarters. But

I didn't know how to find Elias, or if he was even in Constantinople.

So I searched harder for Myrizikos. Patrikia Constanta gave so many parties that Aspasia and I shopped even more than twice a day. Once, coming back from buying fish at Psamatia Harbour, we went inside the Church of the Copper Market where we had seen Irini of Athens. It was built over an old synagogue, Anthusa whispered. I gazed at the gold ceiling and the silver and gold doors that blocked entry to the altar to all but the priest. I stood in the chapel of Saint Soros where the belt of the Mother of God was kept inside a casket locked behind the bars and prayed for Saint Thekla to be returned to me. I prayed before the bones of Saint Zacharias, father to John the Baptist and in the chapel where a miracle-making icon of Christ used to be.

"The monks hid it when icons were banned." Aspasia whispered.

Through those difficult days, I tried to stay optimistic. But sometimes my ear would catch the bleat of a frightened sheep headed for the butcher and a longing for my village would stab my heart like a knife. I would have to stop and drop my head and wait for the pain to pass.

One afternoon, Aspasia and I went out to the point of land overlooking the Propontis Sea and the Golden Horn. We stood on the steps of the Church of Saint Dimitrios and gazed up at the great beacon tower where Emperor Constantine sent flaming coded messages to his armies. Wind ruffled the Propontis Sea just like it ruffled the barley fields of Anatolia. My heart nearly broke for longing. We were not the only ones gazing at the windy sea. The Palace wall is low there and we could see Irini of Athens standing all alone on a terrace. She was staring across the sea to the hills of Bithynia. The wind beat at her cloak but she didn't move.

Aside from those moments of homesickness, my work kept me too busy to be melancholy. Akepsimas sent me to open the gate for the inopios to roll in barrels of wine, or to let in the men who delivered charcoal and wood. I also had to carry the garbage out to the lane. With so many guests, there was too much for the city garbage collectors to take away, so Patrikios Leon hired labourers to carry it to the dump outside the land walls.

And I was learning to cook! I made mustard sauce for pork. I fried sheep brain doused with pepper or mustard. I made proper chickpea soup with pounded chickpeas, or ground them into garlic to make a smooth spread for flat bread. Akepsimas used a wooden mortar for wet foods. "Lemon juice or vinegar ruins a marble mortar," he said.

I stuffed baby goat with garlic, leeks, garum, honey water, and cumin. I crushed almonds in a metal mortar that Akepsimas used only for spices and nuts, and mixed them with almond oil and honey to make a sweet. Akepsimas kept a hoard of expensive spices locked in the spice cupboard but he never told us what he was sprinkling into the pots.

At first, I had thought it was madness for people to eat so much rich food. But the flavours seduced me. I learned to like soft white bread more than barley bread. I liked Aspasia's garum sauce made from the guts of different fish better than my mother's garum made from just river trout. I got used to preparing three-course meals. Patrikia Constanta's household ate meat, chicken, or fish every day except for fast days. They ate cabbage all winter instead of bitter weeds, which we ate in my village. They polished their teeth with a stick of special soft wood from Egypt.

I also learned to cook for each day's religious fast.

"Normally, Patrikia Constanta does not have us strictly follow the fasting laws," explained Aspasia, "but with so many guests who are more devout, she does."

Akepsimas taught me about which days we were permitted to serve. During the forty-day fast before the Feast of the Nativity that ended on January 7, red meat, poultry, eggs, dairy products, fish, oil, and wine were forbidden, although fish, wine and oil were allowed on certain days, I learned how to turn out delicious meals of shellfish, cereals, vegetables and dried fruits so that the forbidden foods were hardly missed.

I didn't know all the religious food laws because we were too poor to have much choice. In my village, we cooked with animal fat and made candles from tallow. We ate two meals a day: millet porridge in the morning and at sunset we had soup or stew of bitter greens, lentils, or cabbage with the occasional bit of pork or mutton.

One Sunday, Aspasia and I walked out to Rymin harbour to treat ourselves to a seafood meal. And there was Elias climbing off a fishing boat dressed in monk's garb. I could not stop my happy cry of welcome. Nor could I stop my tears when he inquired about Myrizikos.

"Saint Thekla will find him," he murmured, patting

my shoulder.

"The Abbess took her." A whisper was all I could manage.

He promptly invited Aspasia and me to a kapelarion and feasted us on steamed clams and fried scallops and fish roe paste that we smeared onto chunks of barley bread and washed down with very good watered wine which Aspasia drank with abandon.

"Where does a monk get money to feed three people at a kapelarion?" she muttered when he went off to pay.

"All I know is I met him on the road to Constantinople," I said, avoiding her eyes.

Elias walked me to the door of Ta Gastria. "I will wait for you at the Milion next Sunday. We will track down that bastard you intend to marry."

"Elias, who exactly are you?" I demanded. "Sometimes you wear a shabby monk's outfit but I saw you in procession dressed better than Patrikios Leon."

"I can't tell you," he said, frankly. "Isn't it enough that we can enjoy each other's company without knowing each other's secrets?"

He would not be waiting for me at the Milion, I was sure. But there he was, dressed like a rich man in a green wool tunica and knotted stockings and tall boots. Aspasia could not join us; she had a sick grandchild, was her excuse.

"It's just the two of us again!" Elias said cheerfully. "Let's go find your soldier."

He bounded off to Dimitrios Point by the beacon tower and pointed down the steep hill to Prosforion Harbour far below and the barges and ferry boats crossing the Golden Horn. "See the tall grain storage towers? See the big iron ring in that cement piling? A massive chain is attached to it. The chain goes under the water of the Golden Horn and is attached to another cement piling on the other side. The chain can be pulled up to stop enemy ships from entering the Golden Horn."

We walked down First Hill to the Golden Horn and asked the guards at every sea gate if they knew a Myrizikos of Ikonion in Anatolia. None had heard of him. Finally we reached the end of the sea walls at Blachernae Palace. I sat on the steps of the church and rubbed my aching feet. I hadn't found Myrizikos. So why was I laughing at every silly remark that Elias made? Why did I smile as he held my hand and helped me onto the little ferry so I wouldn't have to walk all the way back to the convent? We sailed down the Golden Horn and around Saint Dimitrios Point and the beacon tower. He pointed at the broken wall below the Great Palace. "Long ago a mountain of ice floated down the Bosporus Straits and crashed into them," he said.

I climbed out at the harbour below Ta Gastria drenched with sea mist and feeling tired, hungry and I laughed with Elias all the way up the steps to Ta Gastria convent. I hadn't found Myrizikos and yet I was gloriously happy.

***

The banquet that Patrikia Constanta and Akepsimas were giving Co-emperor Leon and Irini his bride was set for mid-November before the Nativity fast began. Every morning, Patrikia Constanta came to the kitchen and told Akepsimas that she wanted to change the menu. Every morning, he refused and she flew into hysterics.

"She is terrified that the imperial couple will go to someone else's party," Megalo told me as I ate her porridge and stewed fruit. She began describing the glorious tunica made of silver thread that Irini of Athens had worn to a party the night before. "She came here without hardly a change of clothing and they were old hand-me-downs. She didn't even have a scarf."

"It blew away on the ship," I said. "I saw it."

"Irini went to Empress Evdokia and asked her to have the Palace tailors make her clothes. The Empress told her that there was no money in the imperial budget for her since she wasn't yet married. So Irini wrote to Emperor Constantine. Right away he ordered the Palace tailors to sew her piles of them. Empress Evdokia was spitting angry."

On banquet day, Akepsimas needed all our help to get the haunch of gazelle spitted and over the fire. I was first to turn the crank. When my back gave out, Akepsimas set me to plucking and cleaning the three ducks that Aspasia had bought that morning, which is a stinking job and hard on the fingers. I cracked the chestnuts and dug out the meat for the stuffing and sauce, which is another mess, and pounded it into chunks with raisins and dried apricots. I stuffed it all into the ducks. I got the turnips and parsnips peeled and boiling and then the morning was over and we were eating leftovers for our mid-day meal.

Then Akepsimas glazed the ducks, sweat dripping off his fleshy cheeks, and put them in the oven. I washed dishes and cranked the spit handle. I could hardly believe the wonderful smells, roasting gazelle, sweet raisins, roast duck.

Before I knew it, the ducks were done and Akepsimas was making the sauce from the drippings with the chestnuts added. I stuck in a finger and swiped a taste. Heaven! Smooth and silky with the chestnut flavour cutting the strong duck taste.

"Keep your fingers out of there!" shouted Akepsimas. Then he smiled. "You'll get your share. I made twice what they will eat."

We sent up the appetizers and Akepsimas carved and plated the meat and vegetables. Sweet Akepsimas, he let each of us up carry up platters so we could see all the glittering jewellery and beautiful clothes. Co-emperor Leon was sitting with the men at one end of the room and Irini of Athens was with the women at the other. She was so beautiful, the other women looked ugly. Her tunica was woven with gold thread. Her gold earrings were shaped like kandilli with sparkling stones for candles. Her hands flashed with rings.

It was past curfew by the time we had cleaned the kitchen so I slept under the table. In the morning, Aspasia woke me and we got the breakfast trays together.

"Irini paints kohl around her eyes," Megalo informed me as I sat on her bed and ate her breakfast. "She paints it on with a tiny brush. She rubs olive oil in her hair to make it shine. Empress Evdokia's hair fell out in chunks after the last baby. My mother told me that the Empress cannot speak about Irini without cursing."

Somehow we got an early supper together for the family and houseguests and Akepsimas sent me home. I was exhausted. The cold air felt good on my hot face.

Snow was settling on the nymphs in the fountain in the Forum of Constantine and on Eleni's shoulders on the Senate steps. I sat down next to her. She looked as tired as me.

"No soldier has heard of your Myrizikos," she yawned. "Of course, they could be lying. I've seen it before. Find another man, sweetie. You're a beautiful young woman. Don't waste your life on this liar."

She left with some soldiers and I sat watching the snow cover the statues of Athena and Zeus. I was too tired to think. I don't know how I got back to the convent and my dormitory bed.

The end of November brought the Brumalia which is my favourite festival. It marks the last of the wine-making, when the liquid from the crushed grapes is fermented and poured into jars. There's lots of drinking raw wine. In my village, we kill a goat, an ancient tradition, because goats eat the vines. I spotted Eleni and some other heteria doing a lively business. Eleni told me that Emperor Constantine was out in the kapelaria and restaurants every night, eating and drinking with his friends. He sent hams and wheels of cheeses to the big public places. Magicians deceived happy audiences. Dancers ran through the streets wearing comic and tragic masks, and musicians played flutes, pipes and lyres. Acrobats in the Forum of Constantine somersaulted high in the air, and jugglers in the Forum of the Ox flung flaming torches even higher.

The Brumalia ends at the winter solstice so before then, the Brumalia parties blend into the Nativity parties. The colonnades along Mesi Street and churches and public buildings fluttered with banners and flags bearing the imperial insignia and the Holy Cross. I watched the Emperor and his family walk in procession to pray at the church at Blachernae Palace before the Veil of the Virgin. An acolyte walked before them carrying the tall gold cross embedded with the Holy and Life-Giving Splinter of the Holy Cross. Patriarch Nikitas ambled behind him. Irini of Athens and Co-emperor Leon wore identical tunicas woven of silver and gold thread. Over them they wore a long purple clamys over one shoulder with a border embroidered with gold. Their scarlet shoes were set with jewels. Kaisar Nikiforos and Kaisar Christoforos wore purple tunicas and clamys.

I walked back to the convent, enjoying the happy crowds in the restaurants and kapelaria. Constantinople had taken my heart. I liked the small lanes where I could escape when Mesi Street was blocked with shoppers or processions. I liked the quiet corners where one lane joined another. I liked the many churches and the tiny flames of oil lamps that burnt inside them all night. I liked smelling the blend of incense, grilled meat, and whiffs of perfume. I liked how people walked quickly and spoke freely. My heart swelled with affection for this overwhelming city that had taken me in.

Still, in the dark winter nights when Aspasia turned off to her apartment and I continued on alone to my convent dormitory bed, I felt the hard truth of my life. I was a young woman alone in a great city seeking a man who wouldn't be found.

Chapter IX

On 17 December Annus Mundi 6260, Irini of Athens, a nobody from the far edge of the empire, wed Leon the Khazak, heir to the throne of the Romans of the East, son of Emperor Constantine and his first wife Tzitzak, grandson of Emperor Leon the Isaurian, first emperor of the Isaurian dynasty. Prince Leon was nineteen. Irini was seventeen.

Megalo gave me the details the following morning while I sat on her bed and ate her breakfast. She lay exhausted against her pillows. "The first ceremony was in the Church of Saint Stephen the Protomartyr in the Palace of Daphne inside the Great Palace. Family only. Irini only had her cousin Theo, so we Friends stood with her. Emperor Constantine's family filled the church. There was him and the Empress and their five sons—Empress Evdokia insisted on bringing baby Anthimos—and Princess Anthusa who was wearing that stinking hair shirt under her silk tunica; I could smell it. Emperor Constantine's three older sisters were there and some of their sons and wives and Empress Evdokia's sister and her husband the army commander and their son. And on and on."

Megalo pointed a limp finger at the warm bread. I dipped it in the honey and handed it to her. She licked off the honey and nibbled on the bread.

"Emperor Constantine couldn't take his eyes off Irini of Athens. She wore a long white tunica and her throat and hair were bound under a blue scarf that was absolutely blinding with silver thread. Patriarch Nikitas prayed forever and Emperor Constantine put the bridal crowns on their heads and said they were wed. Then we all walked in procession across the Augustaion to a big reception hall inside the Great Palace walls. People were absolutely massed in there. Emperor Constantine lifted off their crowns and put on the crowns of Co-emperor and Consort. Patriarch Nikitas prayed more. Then we walked in procession through so many halls and palaces I can't remember them all. Musicians played the lyre and the flute and kithara. The cymbals gave me a headache. Chanters were singing, "God our Saviour, save the rulers! Holy, thrice holy, give them life and health!' Everyone was shouting, 'Many many years!' Which made my headache worse."

She yawned and snuggled into the quilts. "The banquet was in the Hall of Nineteen Couches. I couldn't move for all the people jammed in there and talking at the same time and clashing the gold plates and silver goblets. Everyone said it was the most lavish imperial wedding ever. I'm going back to sleep." She closed her eyes.

Patrikia Constanta's voice came shrieking down the hall. I jumped to my feet and grabbed her tray. The door slammed open. Patrikia Constanta shook Megalo.

"Get up, you lazy girl! Princess Irini can appoint a lady-in-waiting. She's got her own budget as Consort to the Co-emperor. Get over to the Palace and make sure she chooses you. You'll get paid; God knows we need the money after all these guests and parties. You, maid, put down that tray and get her washed and dressed."

Megalo didn't move after her mother slammed out. "Irini isn't going to choose me as her lady-in-waiting, or any of us. She told us she only wants her eunuchs and that mute slave she brought from Athens. She said that we were all Evdokia's spies and the minute she could, she would get rid of all of us."

Parties went on for seven days and nights, and somehow the cooks turned out banquets that still observed the Nativity fast. On January sixth, the evening before the Feast of the Nativity, Patrikios Leon proudly strutted in the procession behind the Emperor from the Great Palace down Mesi Street and up Fourth Hill to pray in the Church of Holy Apostles, then back again to the Hall of the Nineteen Couches for the banquet.

"They will recline to eat like the ancient Romans," Akepsimas told us, rolling his eyes.

"Last year he spilled food all over himself," snickered the laundry maid.

The House Manager sighed. "Let's hope he bribed the Palace official in charge of the banquet door more than last year. He was among the last to be admitted and greeted by the Emperor. So humiliating."

The morning of the Feast of the Nativity on January seventh, all us servants trooped over to stand in the wide Augustaion to watch the Emperor and his family walk from the Great Palace to the Church of Holy Wisdom to attend the Liturgy of St. John Chrysostom and the Divine Liturgy of St. Basil. Then the Emperor went to Magnavra Palace where he sat under the canopy on the gold throne to receive the good wishes of every dignitary and foreign ambassador who could bribe his way in. That evening, the Emperor went to the Church of Holy Wisdom to hear the chanters sing the Old Testament prophecies of Jesus's birth. Or so Megalo told me later. I didn't see any of it. I was up to my elbows in kitchen grease.

After Nativity, there were twelve feast days where everyone went mad eating after the forty days of fasting. Emperor Constantine and his family were walking in a procession every day to some church or going to parties in rich people's houses. We cooked for twenty people on the Feast of the Twenty thousand Martyrs of Nikomidia and I almost burned the fried aubergine, I was so exhausted. When I got back to the convent, it was past curfew and the doors were locked. My boots were soaked through and my feet were numb. I climbed tiredly back up the dark stairs to Mesi Street hoping I could find Aspasia's apartment before the night guards caught me. I was peering into what looked like her alley when a man staggered out of a door near the end and fell against me. My knife was at his throat before I saw who he was.

"Elias!" With relief, I sheathed my knife.

He gingerly felt his throat. "Do I dare ask what you are doing out past curfew?"

I explained, my teeth chattering with the cold.

"Come with me." He drew me down the narrow passage and banged on the door. A peep-hole opened and the door swung wide. A huge bald eunuch stood holding a candle. Behind him a woman lifted her candle.

"Eleni!" I exclaimed.

Elias tossed Eleni a coin. "Give her my room for the night. And warm wine."

I followed Eleni's candle up steep wooden steps. Half-way, she opened a low door into a small and wonderfully warm room. By the light of the glowing coals in the brazier, I could see wood floors covered by heavy rugs, thick curtains pulled against the night, and a bed with a rumpled quilt. Eleni smacked the candle on the table and put her hands on her hips.

"What a liar you are! I was protecting you from my sort of life and you already had clients."

With a sigh I pulled off my soaking cloak and laid it across the drying rack. "Elias and I travelled together from Ikonion. I slept in convents. I thought he was a monk."

"A monk? Elias?" Eleni stared at me. Then she burst out laughing.

I sat on the bed and tried to pull off my boots but they were so wet and I was so tired that I couldn't budge them. Eleni yanked them off and propped them against the brazier where they began to steam.

"So you're the one Elias talks about. He never said

your name."

I peeled off my wet stockings and laid them over a chair. "All I know about Elias is that he has a wealthy aunt in Nicaea. We stayed there two nights."

Eleni flung open the door and shouted for spiced wine. The big eunuch soon appeared with a mug whose sweet aroma filled the room. I drank it straight down. My hands and feet got warm and my head cleared. I pulled my tunica over my head and laid it over the chair. I crawled into the blankets. "Were you sleeping with him?"

"Not me. He doesn't use our services, just the room. He meets people here. Sometimes he sleeps here. When you leave in the morning, be quiet. We sleep late." She stirred up the coals and closed the door.

So my refuge was a brothel. I smiled as I slipped off my damp underclothes and put them over the chair and got back under the heavenly blankets, warm against my bare skin.

After that disaster, I slept under the kitchen table by the warm stove whenever we worked late, like on the Feast of the Holy Innocents and the Feast of the Circumcision. Patrikia Constanta had a dinner party to celebrate the Feast of Saint Basil the Great, which commemorated both the circumcision of Jesus and the Feast day of the Kappadokian Fathers. Then came the feast of the Synaxis of the Seventy and the last feast, Theophany and the Great Blessing of Waters. The Emperor and his family led the procession to the Church of Holy Wisdom to celebrate the baptism of Jesus in the River Jordan and the manifestation of the Holy Trinity. Patrikia Constanta and Patrikios Leon proudly walked behind him with hundreds of dignitaries. All over the empire, priests were blessing people's jugs of water that they then sprinkled over their homes and shops. Patrikia Constanta's house-guests went home.

I was out of a job.

Akepsimas clasped me in his big arms. "I will find you work!" he wept.

But I already had work. Abbess Pulkeria had made me her assistant. She gave me room and board and one follis a week to write letters and keep her daily log and accounts. The first day, she took me into the library where the nuns taught poor girls their letters and numbers. Wax tablets were stacked on the tables. Clothing and blankets were piled against the walls. Abbess Pulkeria looked grim.

"Empress Evdokia wants me to start a scriptorium in here. Other convents have them and she wants one that is bigger and better. She told me to borrow some scrolls and copy them. She's barely literate. She has no idea what this involves. And she has given me no money for supplies." She looked at me.

"What do you want me to do?" I asked cautiously.

"I have two literate nuns who can be spared from their duties for a few hours a week. You are to train them to copy scrolls."

I was horrified. "Abbess, my script is only good for messages and accounts. I am not a calligrapher! I know nothing about copying scrolls."

"You will study in the bookbinding workshop."

Thus began some of the calmest days of my life—

studying to be a scribe under the biblioamphiastis in his tidy workshop behind the Church of Saints Ioannis and Fokas. Every day, I sat at his table and practiced my letters and numbers on wax tablets, surrounded by shelves heavy with scrolls and codices, boxes of quills and bottles of brilliantly coloured inks that he had boiled from plants or nuts or ground from coloured stones.

"The monks of Bithynia buy them for their icons, he whispered, spotting me immediately as a fellow conspirator.

Abbess Pulkeria could not afford those lovely colours, so the bookbinder taught me how to make brown ink by boiling walnut shells and stirring in acacia tree sap and thyme oil to stop mould. He taught me to prepare a parchment page by drawing faint lines across it.

"Your words must not wander about like lost ants," he smiled. "After you have copied an entire scroll, I will sew the parchments together and glue on a leather cover. You will have written a codex, Thekla of Ikonion."

I didn't believe him. But he was a sweet, gentle soul so I worked hard to please him and satisfy Abbess Pulkeria's need to keep Empress Evdokia happy. On my way there, and on the errands that Abbess Pulkeria gave me, I scanned the faces of soldiers for Myrizikos. Abbess Pulkeria assigned me a room in the guest quarters and a place at the guest table, so I slept better and ate meat once a week. I missed the laughter and rich food of Akepsimos's kitchen, but the quiet bookbinding shop soothed my heart which ached from missing Saint Thekla and the peace and ritual of the convent steadied my soul.

When the bookbinder was satisfied with my script, I started work for Abbess Pulkeria. I sat at a table by her study door and wrote letters that she dictated in her even, calm voice. Or I entered convent expenses into a codex that she would present to the bookkeeper at the Palace to prove that she had earned her yearly stipend. Whenever I rested my back and flexed my stiff fingers, my eyes wandered around her study looking for where she might have hidden Saint Thekla. I had not seen any satisfaction on Princess Anthusa's sullen face. Saint Thekla had to be still with Abbess Pulkeria.

My days were not all indoors. I went shopping with the magerissa. She directed the kitchen activities and shopped for provisions. I steered her to better merchants I knew from Aspasia. I bargained well and saved the convent money. My quick knife stopped a pickpocket from getting her purse. After that, Abbess Pulkeria also sent me with the ekonomis when she paid bills. I carried messages from Abbess Pulkeria all over the city. Always, my eyes searched the faces and figures of soldiers for the familiar smile and swinging stride of Myrizikos.

A letter to a convent on Third Hill took me through the Lycus Valley and the slave market—a fearful place where I saw terrified women standing on a platform being auctioned off to shouting bidders. The idea came to me that Myrizikos might have brought slaves here who had been taken prisoner during some battle with the Bulgars. I asked the auctioneer, who told me with a leer that he had not seen any Bulgar prisoners since the Emperor's previous campaign.

Another day, after delivering payment to the fish

market, I went through Pinsos Gate into the Augustaion, planning to ask the guards at Chalke Gate if Myrizikos had finally arrived. Sun blasted off the gold dome of the Church of Holy Wisdom. On impulse, I mounted the church steps and stepped over the high threshold and through the open double doors.

Our village church of Saint Thekla nestles gently against the ground with only one stone step to separate the sacred inner space from the outside world. Bent-over old women with painful joints can step inside to light a candle and murmur a prayer to the bone of Saint Thekla which rests inside a tiny casket in a niche. Not so at the Church of Holy Wisdom. You have to be agile and strong to climb those steep steps and lift your knees over the high threshold. Or rich enough to be carried in a litter.

Darkness in the vast empty space pressed down upon me. During Nativity, the church had been ablaze with candles but today, all was dark and silent. I crept down a side aisle, peering into the chapels dimly lit by narrow windows. My footsteps were swallowed by silence. I fled.

Out in blessed sunshine, I sat on the steps and watched the soldiers guarding Chalke Gate. I felt no need to go and ask about Myrizikos. Something inside me was giving up, and I left.

At the Milion, men were kneeling in the stocks with their necks and wrists locked in the yoke's wooden arms. People were pelting them with rotten food. Stocks were a common enough punishment. I had seen men locked in them in Ikonion. But the stench here and their misery made me feel sick. A shout pulled my eyes to a kapelarion. Eleni! I joined her with relief and called for skewers of grilled pork and shrimp.

"Elias says you aren't working for Patrikios Leon anymore," Eleni said.

I was startled. "How did he know?"

She shrugged. "He knows everything."

I told her about my labours. Neither of us were eager to go back to work so we wandered through the shops in the many stoa at the back of the colonnades along Mesi Street. I found seamstresses, candlemakers, shoemakers, sellers of ribbons and veils, even a shop selling only jewelled cloak-fasteners. I sniffed strange spices from Persia and heady perfumes from Egypt. One shop sold small writing desks. I had seen scribes sitting cross-legged at them in the colonnades writing letters for a coin. I could do the same, I thought. I resolved to save my money and buy a desk.

Mid-February marked forty days after Nativity and the day Christ was presented in the Temple and met Simeon. The full cycle of Nativity feasts was over. I watched beautiful Irini of Athens walk in procession to the Church at Blachernae Palace beside Co-emperor Leon. They walked behind Emperor Constantine but ahead of his other sons. A herd of scarlet-robed bishops shuffled behind them. That night the Emperor would kneel in vigil before the altar. In the morning, he would stand in the church narthex while orphans from the city's orphanages shouted out prayers for his health and safety.

Butcher's Festival comes then and marks the final chariot race until after Easter. In a fit of generosity, Patrikios Leon bought tickets for his servants and Akepsimas talked him into buying one for me. We jammed onto wooden benches at the top of at least thirty rows of seats. Akepsimas pointed to the end of the oval stadium.

"There's Patrikios Leon walking up to the dignitaries box. Now the Emperor's sons are coming out into the covered balcony above the guards. It's called the kathisma. The imperial family comes there from the Palace using special stairs."

Empress Evdokia came waddling out, glittering with gold necklaces and a tunica that must have been entirely silver thread, the way it flashed in the sun.

"And there's our beautiful princess from Athens!" Akepsimas clasped his hands in admiration. "Look how she sparkles! They all have to stand without moving until the Emperor comes. Ah, The Master of Ceremonies is announcing the Emperor."

Emperor Constantine's red and gold robes caught the sunshine. People were rising and cheering.

"The Master of Ceremonies is lifting the tip of the Emperor's cloak, his chlamys," Akepsimas explained. "He is making a fold. He places it into the Emperor's hand. See? Now the Emperor is lifting the chlamys and making the sign of the cross. The races can begin!"

A low wall ran down the centre of the racecourse. On it rose a pillar that came to a point at the top. Another pillar looked like snakes climbing a pole.

"That wall is the spina," Akepsimas explained. "See the seven statues of dolphins at one end? And the seven eggs at the other end? Every time the first chariot passes a dolphin or an egg, an attendant removes one. That's how we keep track of the seven rounds."

Horses and chariots burst from starting stalls and thundered around the spina. An attendant removed a dolphin. Irini of Athens waved her arms and jumped up and down. The dust-covered winner stopped below the kathisma, the Emperor handed down the prize, and we settled back to chat before the next race.

After the fourth race, men in bright coloured tunicas and caps came out and began to sing and dance in rhythm. Akepsimas sang the refrain along with everyone. "Behold, sweet spring is rising again, bringing health and life and prosperity, courage from God to the Emperor of the Romans, and a God-given victory over the enemy!"

My heart overflowed with love and gratitude to our emperor who protected and loved us. I shouted out with everyone, "Many upon many years!"

Lenten fasting began. I waited in the long line to the Church of Holy Wisdom to kiss the Holy and Life-Giving Splinter of the Holy Cross that the priests put out for six days. Then came the celebration of the first and second finding of the Head of Saint John the Forerunner. Emperor Constantine and his family led the procession out the Golden Gate to the Church of John the Baptist seven miles away in Evdomon, a fishing village and army training ground. Aspasia and I decided to follow the procession. It was a lovely spring day and a chance for fresh air and a view beyond city walls.

"Myrizikos could be riding in the Emperor's personal guard today," Aspasia said cheerfully as we watched the acolytes pass carrying the tall standards with the flags emblazoned with the imperial crest and the Holy Cross.

The Emperor's guard rode by on their beautiful horses. My breath caught. Was that Myrizikos? His helmet hugged the sides of his face and covered his brow. I stepped forward as he came nearer. His eyes flicked at me and then flicked away. Had I had found him? Was that recognition in the soldier's eye? But where was my surge of happiness? I felt nothing. What should I do, I thought. If I ask for him at Chalke Gate, the guards will say he isn't there.

I barely felt myself dip my knee and bow as the carriage passed with Patriarch Nikitas. I barely felt myself kneel as Emperor Constantine rode by on his white charger. I was silent as Aspasia and I walked out the Golden Gate.

"You saw your soldier, didn't you?" demanded Aspasia.

"I'm not sure."

She squeezed my arm. "Find another lad. This one is wed to the Emperor."

I tried to put Myrizikos out of my mind as we strolled along the windy sea. When we got to Evdomon, the ceremony was over and the Emperor's family and favourites were jammed into kapelaria. We wandered around looking for an empty table. There were none anywhere. Then who should call my name but Elias! He was wearing a tunica of deep indigo with yellow leggings and leather shoes.

"He's not a monk!" Aspasia hissed, hiding her mouth under her scarf.

"Not always," I muttered. We hurried to the table that a kapelarios had suddenly discovered was available. Soon we were devouring the mussels and scallops that

Elias kept ordering hot off the grill.

I told him about my studies to be a calligrapher and how I was teaching the nuns at Ta Gastria to copy scrolls. Aspasia gossiped about Megalo and how her betrothed, Fanis, ignored her when he and his mother came for supper. Elias's banter made me laugh as we walked the seven cold miles back to Ta Gastria.

I hurried in at dusk just as the novice was closing the gate and stumbled over a stone flower pot, gashing my shin. The hospice nun bandaged it and the next day I went about my duties. But by evening the scrape was fire hot and dripping pus. The hospice nurse bandaged it again but a dull ache kept me awake. In the morning, my leg stank like a dead sheep. I could put no weight on it. The magerissa hurried to bring a litter to take me to Sampson Hospital.

"All the rich people go to Sampson," Abbess Pulkeria assured me as I climbed in, shivering and sweating, my leg stabbing with pain. "The doctor for Princess Irini is head physician."

Two medical assistants carried me inside the big stone hospital behind the Church of Holy Wisdom. The xenodohos admitted me straight to a bed in the women's ward. Around me women were moaning in pain or lying frighteningly still. There was a wall that didn't reach the vaulted ceiling. I could hear men groaning on the other side. I looked up at the dirty windows high on the walls and thought about the farmer in my village who had died after a ram had stepped on his leg. Was the soothsayer in the Ikonion pig market right? Would I die alone far from home? Saint Thekla couldn't save me. She was gone.

A cool hand on my hot forehead woke me. Gentle hands unwrapped the bandages. A man with dark hair and eyes and a kind, quiet voice told me he was Doctor Moses and that he was going to cure my leg. He spoke Greek with an odd accent. Two women hypourgia lifted my shoulders while a man who said he was Andreas held a cup of sticky sweet liquid to my lips.

"Poppy seed medicine," he coaxed. "It will take away the pain."

"Will I lose my leg?" I whispered. "Will I die?"

"You will recover and soon be back at work," Doctor Moses replied cheerfully. "Rot has set in but we will take care of that straightaway."

My eyes grew heavy and I felt nothing until I awoke in the dark, soaked in sweat and my leg throbbing with pain. I reached for Saint Thekla. Some moments passed before I remembered she was gone. A sob of despair escaped me. Warm hands clasped mine.

"It's Aspasia, my dear. Abbess Pulkeria sent a message that you were here."

Tears spilled hot on my cheeks. "My leg is rotting," I whispered. "I have lost Saint Thekla and I will die."

"The saints don't desert those who are faithful," Aspasia said stoutly. "They have sent the bees to cure you. Honey is curing your wound. Doctor Moses says our Greek ancestors used it for deep wounds. He has had great success."

She lifted my head. In the faint light by a distant candle, I could see that a heavy bandage wrapped my leg. She dipped her finger in a small jar and touched my lips. The sweetness brought me no comfort, such was my despair at losing Saint Thekla and her protection. Aspasia put a cup to my lips.

"Drink this. Doctor Moses wants you to have some whenever you wake up."

I choked down the sickening sweet brew. When next I awoke, doves were fluttering and cooing on the high windows ledges. A faint pink light meant dawn. I had been dreaming that I was clasping Saint Thekla to my heart and an extraordinary peace wrapped me like soft wool. I lay very still, trying to hold the marvellous feeling but it faded and the heavy ache in my leg returned. I shifted to ease the pain. Aspasia came quickly. She held the cup to my lips. Again I slept.

This time I dreamed that Princess Anthusa was standing over me. The dream so frightened me that I opened my eyes. The princess was indeed standing by my bed. She was holding her scarf over her mouth and nose.

"Abbess Pulkeria said you were ill. I came to pray for you."

"Pray that God will forgive your lies. You took Saint Thekla from me. Now I will die."

"I don't have her. Abbess Pulkeria won't give her to me."

"You broke your promise not to tell her." I turned my face away, consumed by pain.

"I told the abbess for your own sake. I wanted her to know the strength of your faith."

"Liar! You wanted Saint Thekla for yourself."

Women were turning their heads. Princess Anthusa lowered her voice to a hiss. "Do not speak to me like this. I will have your tongue slit."

"Go ahead. My leg is rotting and I will die."

Princess Anthusa's shoulders slumped. "May God forgive me for breaking my word."

"God will not forgive you and neither will I." I closed my eyes and fell into a deep sleep.

I dreamed that Elias was standing by me wearing a tunica of deep green with white leggings and tall red leather boots polished to a shine. His cloak was lined with blue silk. He was talking to Doctor Moses. They embraced. I tried to call out to him but, as in dreams, my voice made no sound and he left without looking back.

Aspasia slept every night on a mat by my bed. She held the poppy-seed medicine to my lips every time I awoke. In the morning, she went to work and Akepsimas brought foods to help me heal—boiled eggs, bread kneaded with mastic, chickpea stew. He brought dates filled with almonds and slices of fried cracked wheat porridge.

Alone all day, I lay in a fog of pain and poppy-seed medicine. I watched the doctors and the hypourgia bathe wounds, apply leeches and poultices, administer potions and medicines. Sampson Hospital was a city in itself. Before my drugged eyes passed laundresses, cooks and bakers, cauldron keepers, grooms for the doctors' horses, gate keepers, pursers, pall bearers, millers, latrine cleaners. A scribe carried a small writing desk among the beds and wrote letters for a coin.

"I could gain some income by writing letters," I said to Aspasia. "But I need a writing desk." A hopeless feeling came over me when I remembered the price of the small writing desk I had seen in the shop.

Doctor Moses or Andreas checked my wound several times a day, sniffing it, prodding the skin around it, feeling it for heat. Their kind smiles healed me as much as the honey and poppy seed drink. Andreas began lingering to chat. He had a pleasant voice and his visits were a welcome change from the boredom of my days.

"Sampson is a better hospital than Evbouilos Hospital, or even Saint Irini in Perama Hospital, he bragged. "It is even better than Saint Panteleimon Hospital or Christodotes Hospital. Each hospital has its own doctors. Doctor Moses is the protarch, the chief of staff. Under him are the physicians and the junior physicians. Each level trains the next. Doctor Moses works six months here and six months in his own clinic. The Palace pays him when he is here, and all the staff. Doctors earn very little in the hospital—less than the minimum wage for day labourers. But it's a prestigious position and good experience. They gain private patients. Princess Irini is Doctor Moses' patient," he added proudly. "She often summons him to the Palace."

"Is she sick?" I asked, in my weakened state distressed that the beautiful princess might be taken from us.

"Oh no," he smiled. "They are old friends. She likes his company."

Doctor Moses wore simple tunicas of rough wool in plain dark red or blue, and serviceable boots, not like the fancy clothes of the doctors under him. He spoke to them with the same polite courtesy as he spoke to the fisherwoman in the next bed. He had removed an infected fishhook from her hand.

"What is Doctor Moses's accent?" I asked Andreas.

"He is from Antioch, in the Caliphate. He was a deacon in the Church of Antioch and a prominent physician. He was actually the personal physician for Caliph al-Mansur."

"Why did he come here?"

Andreas lowered his voice. "Doctor Moses told me he had attended the child who was heir to the throne. The child went into a coma. So the elders named Caliph al-Mansur's own son to be heir. A rumour went around that Doctor Moses had given the child a drug that put him in the coma. Doctor Moses needed to get out of Antioch quickly. A monk from the Office of the Eparch of Monasteries had just came to inspect the monasteries. He got Doctor Moses on a ship to Thessaloniki. He opened a clinic there. When Princess Irini got sick coming from Athens, she went to his clinic. He cured her."

I remembered what Auntie Sofia had said about Irini being ill in Thessaloniki. "What was wrong with her?"

He shrugged. "I don't know. But the princess was so grateful that she asked Emperor Constantine to bring him to Constantinople and give him a position at Sampson Hospital. The doctor bought a compound in the Copper Market for his clinic. He has a nurse and housekeeper and a few beds for private patients. I live there." he added with a proud smile.

Andreas asked me about myself. Weak in body and spirit, I told the truth about Myrizikos. He looked at me with a confused frown.

"Two years have passed since you were betrothed. Under the law, you are free. Why do you not find a better husband? There must be many young men eager to marry you."

I couldn't answer.

The pain in my leg eased and I needed no more poppy-seed drink. The tight bandage kept the honey in place so I could stand up to wash myself and move to the latrine behind the building. One day, Elias arrived wearing his rich man's clothes. He placed on my lap a gleaming wooden box.

"A writing table!" I gasped. Overwhelmed, I put my scarf over my face and sobbed. "Who are you, Elias, that you can afford such a gift?"

"What does it matter who we are on the outside? It is our soul that counts. Now you can write letters for other patients. Open the lid."

Inside were partitions with quills and ink and a drawer with papyrus sheets.

He pulled up a stool and told me the news. "Emperor Constantine has ordered Patriarch Nikitas to start rebuilding churches that were damaged by earthquakes. Many have been in disgraceful condition since Emperor Leon's time. Patriarch Nikitas is taking the opportunity to remove any mosaic images of Christ and the saints."

"No surprise," I shrugged.

"The Caliph's commanding general Banakas has invaded and taken prisoners."

"What else is new?" I sighed.

"Commander Mihalis the Dragon has rounded up all the monks and nuns in Ephesus and ordered them to choose whether to marry or suffer blinding and exile to Cyprus."

"Stop!" I put my hands over my ears. "Is there no good news?"

"News is always good for someone." He patted my feet and sauntered out. I caught a glimpse of him talking to Doctor Moses before I busied myself sharpening quills.

The very next day, Doctor Moses took a sniff of my wound and announced, "The rot is gone. Let us see if the wound is healed."

Andreas brought over a cart loaded with basins, sponges, and pitchers of warm water. The honey washed off without pain and there was my leg, good as new except for a scar.

"Go home," smiled Doctor Moses. "The saints and the bees have healed your leg." There was no fee. Elias had paid, Andreas told me.

Andreas walked me to the Church of Saint Irini. Under the gold and silver dome, I lit a candle before the little casket holding the saint's finger bone. "Dear Saint Irini, thank you for healing me. Please tell Saint Thekla that I miss her and I long for her return," I prayed.

I was too weak to walk to Ta Gastria so Andreas paid for a litter. Abbess Pulkeria sent me straight to bed and the cook brought me oxtail soup and rye bread. A day's rest in the courtyard sun and I was back at my desk entering numbers into the accounts codex and supervising the nuns copying scrolls in the scriptorium. Another week and I was delivering letters and messages.

One day I was in a shop with the magerissa who was buying linen. Irini of Athens and her Friends were buying silk. The shopkeeper slid her gaze over the slim figure of the princess.

"Not yet with child. She better get herself pregnant or she will find herself back in Athens," she said, shaking her head soberly.

Chapter X

Pink almond tree blossoms scented the courtyard of Ta Gastria. I took my writing desk to different hospitals and wrote letters for the sick for an occasional coin. On Wednesdays, I met Eleni at the Old Golden Gate bathhouse and we exchanged news while we were being scrubbed. On Sundays, Aspasia and I went for seafood at Rymin fishing village. One Sunday, Andreas was with her.

"You arranged this," I said to Aspasia. She laughed.

We found a table and ordered steamed mussels and grilled shrimp. Not far away, Princess Irini was laughing and talking with her cousin and other richly-dressed men and women. I could hear her strong Athens accent ordering dish after dish. Her face was flushed with wine and the brisk sea breeze. Her belted tunica showed she was still slim.

On Great Tuesday during Holy Week before Easter,

Emperor Constantine led the procession to the Church of Holy Apostles. Behind him walked Co-emperor Leon and Consort Irini with Leon's three half-brothers and legions of scarlet-robed bishops. On Great Thursday, again I saw her in procession dropping coins into the wrinkled hands of old people who lived in the public gerokomia, the old people's homes, and in the public poorhouses. On Great Friday, I saw her and Leon in a carriage behind the Emperor's carriage going to the church at Blachernae Palace where the Emperor would keep vigil before the altar until midnight on Saturday. On Easter day the Emperor sat on his golden throne accepting the good wishes of every dignitary and foreign ambassador.

Lilies bloomed in the flowerpots of Ta Gastria. Cherry and apricot trees snowed scented white blossoms over the courtyard. I left my window open at night and heard the soft chanting of the contemplative nuns. It was sweet but what my heart longed for was the cry of the owl and the murmurs of drowsy sheep. Walking up Mesi Street, I raised my eyes to the thin strip of blue sky between the tall buildings and a desperate longing came over me to see the horizon. I walked out to Saint Dimitrios Point by the beacon tower. Ships were passing in and out of the Golden Horn. Some sailed up the Bosporus to the Pontus Sea, others towards the Dardanellia and Thessaloniki. Still others blew towards the prison islands that Elias had named. Waves rolled over the Propontis Sea but instead of their blue water, my aching heart saw soft tall grasses bending before the winds of Anatolia.

One morning, Princess Anthusa burst into Abbess Pulkeria's study, a small awkward figure in a long rough-weave tunica of undyed linen and ugly rough sandals. Abbess Pulkeria and I rose and bent our knees. Anthusa's high voice was shrill with excitement.

"My mother has summoned Abbess Anthusa of Mantinia. She will stay here."

Abbess Pulkeria clasped her hands and beamed like I had never seen her. "Thanks be to God! I have not seen my dear Anthusa for years." Fear flickered over her serene face. "Why is the Empress summoning her? Is the Empress ill?"

The answer burst out in a flood of anger. "Horrid Irini of Athens claims she is with child! She lies! Abbess Anthusa is coming to discover the truth. The Abbess will arrive in a few days. Send a messenger immediately. An imperial litter will come for her." Her sandals clattered out the gate.

Abbess Pulkeria sank onto a couch and crossed herself. Her face had gone white. I ran for the nursing sister who hurried back with a cup of warm syrup of drakani flowers. After some moments, the Abbess's colour returned.

"Poor Princess Anthusa," she murmured, shaking her head. "Her jealousy is taking her over. This will lead only to sorrow."

"Can Abbess Anthusa really say if Irini of Athens carries a child?" I asked.

"God willing. She predicted that Empress Evdokia would have healthy twins. You know the story?"

"Empress Evdokia became very ill when she was carrying Princess Anthusa."

"She was close to death. The doctors could do noth-

ing. Emperor Constantine summoned Abbess Anthusa."
Abbess Pulkeria lowered her voice. "Emperor Constantine was in trouble. His first two wives had died in childbirth. He had just locked three hundred and thirty-three bishops inside Hieria Palace until they banned icons as heresy. Monks were shouting in the streets that God had sent the Angel of Death to take Empress Evdokia as punishment for banning icons. The Emperor was losing the loyalty of the army. He feared for his throne.

"Sister Anthusa was known for her miracles. She had a huge following. She refused to stop praying before icons and was causing rebellions all over the Empire. The Emperor had her branded with hot irons—some say he pressed the red-hot metal into her body himself. She felt no pain. Witnesses called her a saint."

Abbess Pulkeria lowered her voice further. "Emperor Constantine is a cunning, devious, manipulator. He needed to gain back the loyalty of the army if he was to keep the throne. He could do this by showing that he believed in our orthodox tradition of miracle healing. So he summoned Abbess Anthusa. He had nothing to lose. If she performed a miracle, he would bow before her in gratitude and gain the loyalty of the army and the monks both. If she could not, he would call her an instrument of the devil and have her executed and out of his hair. Anthusa put her hands on the empress's belly and predicted that she would birth a healthy son and daughter—twins. Which she did. The Emperor gave Anthusa a double imperial convent in Mantinia on the Pontus Sea. He pays her from the imperial budget."

"But now she is at the beck and call of the Empress,"

I noted.

Abbess Pulkeria sighed. "Unfortunately, yes. Now it appears that Empress Evdokia wants her to predict whether Irini of Athens is carrying a child, or if she is lying. This can only lead to disaster—for Irini of Athens or for Abbess Anthusa."

"I have seen her out shopping. The belt of her tunica fits as tight as mine. What will happen to her if Abbess Anthusa says that she is not with child?"

Abbess Pulkeria tightened her lips grimly. "Empress Evdokia will accuse her of lying to her husband. This is grounds for divorce and exile. Even execution."

I gaped at her. "Emperor Constantine wouldn't do that. He chose Irini of Athens as his son's bride. He brought her on his warship."

"He will honour Evdokia's request. She has given him five healthy sons and shows no sign of stopping. Women all over the empire revere her. Men, as well. She is proof of the Emperor's youthful loins."

"Why is Empress Evdokia being so vengeful?" I asked, but I knew as soon as I spoke the words.

"Empress Evdokia had planned to marry her niece to Co-emperor Leon. She is determined to break this marriage and get her niece married to the heir. Then her niece will be empress when Leon becomes emperor after the Emperor dies."

"What if Abbess Anthusa says that Irini of Athens is indeed with child?"

"Abbess Anthusa will be taking a big risk. Empress Evdokia could tell the Emperor to have the charter of the convent at Mantinia revoked and have the abbess sent into exile. It is not easy to serve both God and the crown."

Some days later, Abbess Anthusa strode into the gates accompanied by two nuns and two monks. She was a tiny old woman with a deeply wrinkled face that peeked out from a tightly wrapped maforion. Her linen tunica and full trousers were dusty and her sandals were well-worn. Abbess Pulkeria flung herself on her knees and kissed the hem of the little Abbess's tunica, as did we all. One novice went running for water, another for sweet watered wine, another for bread and olives. Others went for basins of water to bathe her feet.

Me, I took the two monks to find lodging at Saint Andrew Salus Monastery across Mesi Street. But first, I showed them to the Old Golden Gate bathhouse and urged them to visit the waters as soon as possible. Then, with leaden feet, I trudged to the Palace to tell Princess Anthusa that the famed Abbess had arrived. Soon, slim Princess Irini would stand before this all-knowing abbess and be pronounced either mother or liar.

The guard at Chalke Gate told me to wait. I went over and sat in the shade by the door to the silk factory. A week had passed since I had last asked the guards at Chalke Gate if they knew Myrizikos of Ikonion. I had got the usual rude answer. I watched people climb the steps to the Church of Holy Wisdom. A certain calm clarity came over me, like when a river slows its rush and the water becomes clear to the bottom. I sat motionless, not seeing, not hearing, just feeling that clarity. Something inside me was making a decision.

A boot kicked my leg. A guard pointed at some bearers

carrying a litter out Chalke Gate flanked by four guards. Princess Anthusa was going to Ta Gastria. I walked back though the side lanes to Ta Gastria. I took my time and loitered at my favourite shops. The litter bearers had to fight the crowds on Mesi Street. I sniffed the pungent spices and sweet perfumes. I fingered soft silks. I felt the clarity filling me like cool rain fills a cistern.

When I got back to the Abbess's study, Princess Anthusa was standing before Abbess Anthusa who was sitting placidly on a couch. The little Abbess had washed and put on a clean tunica. She looked as fresh as if she had risen from a night's sleep. Princess Anthusa had her hands folded meekly like a postulant, but her jaw was set in a rebellious scowl. Abbess Pulkeria motioned me to stand just inside the door.

"My dear Princess Anthusa," Abbess Anthusa said to her namesake, "Please explain why your mother has summoned me."

"My half-brother's wife, Irini of Athens, claims that she carries his child. You must place your hands on her belly and tell us the truth."

"Does a woman not know when she is with child?"

"Irini is lying. She constantly lies. Every word from her lips is a lie."

"Why would she lie about carrying a child?" The Abbess's voice remained patient.

"She lies because if she is barren, Leon can divorce her."

"It has not been even a year since they were wed. She is young. There is time."

Anthusa flushed. "My half-brother has not entered

175

Irini's bedchamber since their wedding night. All the Palace eunuchs say so."

I stiffened. I felt Abbess Pulkeria do the same. Abbess Anthusa raised her eyebrows.

"Why does he not enter her chamber? I hear she is beautiful and has a quick mind."

Princess Anthusa twisted her fingers. "Leon was once betrothed to Gisela, daughter of King Pepin of the Franks. The betrothal was broken off. Leon still dreams of being king of the Franks."

"Has the Emperor indicated that this marriage to Gisela might still happen?"

"Gisela has entered a convent."

Abbess Anthusa regarded her thoughtfully. "If I understand you, my child, Empress Evdokia has summoned me to ask God if Consort Irini of Athens is with child—even though servants say that Co-emperor Leon has not lain with her."

"Yes, Abbess," she said, eagerly.

"What if God tells me that the Consort is indeed with child?"

"Then the bastard is not Leon's! You must name the father! The Emperor will have this traitor executed. Irini will be sent to that prison convent in Lesbos!" Her voice rang with triumph.

The Abbess's voice remained smooth. She addressed the small quivering fifteen-year-old. "Does your mother have any idea whose child this might be?"

Words burst forth. "Her cousin Theo. He came with her from Athens. They are together always, even in her bedchamber."

"Any other candidates?" The old woman's voice was dry.

"A young army captain called Elpidios. He comes often to her chambers."

"Anyone else? We hear rumours, even in Mantinia."

"My mother says . . ." Princess Anthusa stopped. She swivelled her head and glared at me.

Abbess Anthusa said smoothy. "No words will leave this room. What does your esteemed mother say?"

"That my father had carnal knowledge of Irini on the warship when he brought her from Athens. He still visits that harlot's bedchamber! He sends her guard away. He leaves deep in the night. All the eunuchs say so."

Abbess Pulkeria became as still as stone. I could not breathe. Abbess Anthusa's serene face showed no surprise. "Child, think deeply before you answer. What if God tells me that no child grows inside her womb. What then?"

Princess Anthusa smiled. "Leon will divorce her. He will send her to that prison convent on Lesbos. He will wed my mother's niece, as my mother had planned before my father brought this harlot from Athens."

The little Abbess's eyebrows rose again. "Co-emperor Leon has agreed to wed this niece? What of his dream of being king of the Franks?"

"I don't know," Princess Anthusa mumbled.

The Abbess sat watching her for a long time. "Let us say for the moment that Princess Irini is with child and remains the consort of Co-emperor Leon. Let us say, God forbid, that Emperor Constantine dies. Princess Irini will become Empress Irini. Empress Evdokia must then leave the Palace. This is what usually happens to the widows of emperors, is it not?"

"Yes, Abbess."

"But if Co-emperor Leon marries the niece of Empress Evdokia, the Empress will remain in the Palace. She will keep all her wealth and privileges. Yes?"

"Yes, Abbess, probably." Princess Anthusa stared at the floor.

"And you will remain at the Palace with all your privileges."

"I don't want any privileges! I will take the vows when my father dies. I will become a contemplative nun and spend my life in prayer."

The Abbess nodded thoughtfully. "Please inform Empress Evdokia that I will pray for guidance. When God has prepared me, I will come to the Palace."

"But Abbess, my mother is waiting for you now!"

Abbess Anthusa rose. Without another word, she went out the door and across the courtyard. She entered the narrow door to the abaton where the contemplative nuns lived. The door closed behind her.

A week passed, and two. One warm morning when I came back from shopping with the ekonomis, I found Abbess Anthusa sitting in Abbess Pulkeria's study sipping a mug of mountain tea. Abbess Pulkeria was behind her desk.

"Thekla," she said with a cautious glance at Abbess Anthusa smiling placidly from the couch. "Abbess Anthusa wants you to accompany her to the Palace. You will wait for her and you will bring her back. I have sent a message that she is coming."

"Why me?" I was astounded.

Abbess Anthusa answered. "My child, Abbess Pulkeria has spoken of your devotion to God and your strength of purpose. And your knowledge of this great city. You can show me the sights. I have always wanted to see Constantinople."

For such an old woman, Abbess Anthusa was agile and strong of leg. She was also enormously curious. We walked slowly because she was fascinated by all her eye fell upon—the scribes writing letters in the colonnades, the fancy shops and food markets. We rested in the Forum of the Ox and again in the Forum of Constantine so she could watch the people.

Princess Anthusa was waiting impatiently with her guards outside Chalke Gate. She wore a long dull-green tunica and had wrapped her hair, throat, forehead and chin in undyed linen, like a nun. I could smell the rank odour of her hair shirt. "Wait here," she ordered me.

"She comes with me." Abbess Anthusa gripped my arm.

We passed through white stone palaces, shady gardens, and marble archways, all so glorious that my eyes could hardly believe they were real. We climbed the broad steps of a white stone palace bounded by white marble pillars. Guards opened the wide double doors. Inside were courtyards open to the sky and wide passageways lined with doors. Finally a eunuch in a white tunica opened some double doors.

Before me lay a long room with a wall of doors open to a garden. Women wearing colourful tunicas and glittering scarves were sitting on thick cushions on deep carpets, chattering like bright birds as they ate off small plates. Servants moved about with platters of fruit, sliced meat and cheeses, and small pastries. My stomach rumbled. I spotted Patrikia Constanta, who stared at me with her mouth open.

Empress Augusta Evdokia sprawled on a wide couch on a raised platform at the end of the room. Her purple tunica was askew and her bare feet stuck out. Henna reddened her thin hair and her skin gleamed with creams. She was shoving pastries into her mouth from a platter balanced on her large belly. A servant stood beside her holding a tray with a large glass goblet.

Princess Irini sat very erect on a couch to the left of the platform. Near her sat Megalo and her other two Friends, Tisti and Doti. I knew them from Patrikia Constanta's parties. Megalo smiled at me and gave me a tiny wave. But my attention was on the beautiful princess. Not a wrinkle showed in the princess's blue tunica with its front panel of embroidered flowers. Loose green trousers skimmed jewelled sandals. A long yellow scarf lay casually about her neck. Large pearl earrings mingled with her thick hair. The eunuch at the door rapped his staff.

"Princess Anthusa! Abbess Anthusa of Mantinia!"

Two eunuchs hoisted the empress upright. They jammed gold sandals on her feet and got her standing. They eased her off the dais. Her purple silk tunica spread about her like a giant tent.

"Welcome, Amma Anthusa," she said in a thick heavy voice using the religious title of respect. "Come forward." Her voice was thick and heavy.

There was a rush of silk as every woman flung herself face down on the floor. I started to step backwards out the door but Abbess Anthusa tightened her grip. Together, we walked through the women kneeling on both sides of us. Abbess Anthusa murmured soft blessings. We stopped in front of Empress Evdokia. I quickly backed away and dropped flat in full prostration.

Hearing heavy breathing, I lifted my head to see what was going on. Empress Evdokia was trying to bend her knees to kiss the hem of the abbess's tunica. Her bulk wouldn't allow it. With a grunt, she waved vaguely at the hem and touched her lips with her fingers, then she engulfed the tiny nun in her great arms and kissed her cheeks. She stepped back and wriggled her fingers. Everyone rose with more rush of silk and whispers. She lifted her arms and her eunuchs hoisted her back on the dais. She settled, wheezing, her elbows resting on her splayed-out knees like a giant purple frog. She waved a casual hand towards Princess Irini, standing with her hands folded.

"Irini of Athens, consort of Co-emperor Leon."

Irini gracefully sank flat on the floor in a full prostration achieved in a motion as smooth as water flowing over a stone.

"Rise, my child," murmured Abbess Anthusa.

Irini rose to her knees. She kissed the hem of the abbess's tunica then stood without any visible effort. Her clear, light voice carried her Athens accent down the long room.

"It is an honour to be in your presence, Abbess Anthusa. In Athens, we spoke often of your miracles."

"God's miracles." The Abbess took both of the Princess's hands and drew her to the couch. They sat facing each other. From where I was standing, I could see their faces and hear their voices clearly. The room was still while everyone strained to hear.

"I am told you are with child, my dear," the abbess said gently.

"Thanks be to God." Princess Irini delicately removed one of her hands and crossed herself. She leaned forward and her voice took on a confidential tone. Still, her voice was loud enough to carry down the long room. "Abbess Anthusa, may I make a confession?"

A faint gasp floated over the room. Empress Evdokia grunted as she leaned her huge body forward to hear better. Princess Irini of Athens gazed into the abbess's eyes. "Last night I had a dream. A voice like no other came into my ears. It was the clear sweet voice of a woman. Could this be a saint, Abbess Anthusa?"

"It is possible, my child. What did the voice say?"

Princess Irini gazed upward to the ceiling with a wondering look. She waited so long that I became dizzy from holding my breath. "The clear sweet voice said, 'Irini of Athens, you bear inside your womb a healthy male Isaurian.'"

Empress Evdokia made a strangling sound.

Irini smiled sweetly at the little Abbess. "What do you suppose is the meaning of this dream, Abbess Anthusa?"

Abbess Anthusa leaned forward and spoke so softly that had I not been so near and had my eyes not been fixed on her lips, I would not have known her words. "Do not tempt fate, my child."

Irini's reply was equally quiet. "Who can know our fate? Surely not a humble abbess."

Abbess Anthusa rose and faced Empress Evdokia. "O Worthy Empress, during these weeks of deep prayer, I have asked God for an answer to your request. God has now granted my prayer. You have His answer before you in the words of a saint who visited your daughter-in-law in a dream."

The empress sputtered. Bits of spittle flew from her lips. "You cannot believe this lie, surely. The little sponger is making it up!"

Abbess Anthusa remained calm. "Empress, begging your pardon, but no good Christian woman would risk the wrath of God by pretending to hear the words of a saint."

Princess Irini smiled serenely.

Empress Evdokia beat her hands on the couch in fury. "She is not the daughter-in law I wanted!"

"'Daughter-in-law, not as you know but as you find,'" the little abbess replied, quoting the old saying. "Now, I beg you to grant me leave. I have duties in Mantinia. I have been gone far too long."

"Wait! Dine with us!" Empress Evdokia beckoned frantically at the eunuchs who were holding the trays of food. "Stay, Abbess Anthusa. The Emperor wants to greet you. It has been too many years."

"Your Grace, a Higher Power calls me back to my responsibilities. It is a journey of three days and I must get started."

The eunuchs got the empress off her dais. Again she kissed her fingers and waved at the Abbess's hem. Abbess Anthusa beckoned to me and took my arm. As we turned, my eyes met the dark eyes of Princess Irini of Athens. The princess's mouth was solemn but those beautiful eyes were laughing.

Princess Anthusa walked with us to Chalke Gate. There, the little Abbess took the Princess's hands. "Do not underestimate Irini of Athens, my dear child. She will make a better friend than enemy."

For once, Princess Anthusa had nothing to say.

I sighed with relief when we were by the Milion and surrounded by the familiar noise of Mesi Street. The Abbess lifted her nose. "Is that grilled shrimp? Do you have coins for a meal? I'm absolutely famished."

I was so astounded that I blurted out the thought had been tumbling through my head. "Abbess, did Irini of Athens really have that dream?"

The Abbess smiled. "My child, God did not grant me the gift of prescience so that I could satisfy the conniving of an empress. Either God sent Irini of Athens a dream, or God gave her a clever mind and set her free to use it. Either way, her dream saved me from having to refuse the Empress's command."

"She is so beautiful," I sighed.

"'From the thorn springs the rose and from the rose the thorn,' is the old saying. Irini of Athens is clever. She has courage. But her strengths will become her weaknesses, if she is not careful. Good and evil live in our hearts, my child. God lets us choose which to hold and which to release. I will pray that Irini of Athens chooses wisely. Now here is a nice kapelarion. Let us eat."

I was so flustered that I ordered far too many grilled shrimp and chickpea paste smeared on grilled flatbread.

The abbess devoured it as if she hadn't eaten in days.

"Abbess Pulkeria tells me you search for your betrothed," she said through full mouth.

I drank my watered wine and replied with absolute certainty, even as sadness washed over me and settled in the place where hope had died. "I have given up my search. Myrizikos does not want to be found. Abbess, why does God let men abandon us at the altar and go away with no punishment? Myrizikos will lose only the betrothal gift. I am now called used goods."

"God was not consulted when men made the law," she said grimly. Then she patted my hand. "Abbess Pulkeria has told me of your devotion to Saint Thekla of Ikonion."

I looked at her sharply.

"Your icon is waiting for you, child. The abbess keeps her word. Your devotion to your saint tells me that you may find a full life in Ta Gastria convent," she added.

I put my hands over my face, overwhelmed by tears of relief. I wiped my eyes. "I live at Ta Gastria because it is safe, Abbess. Not because I wish to join the convent."

"Come to Mantinia on retreat. God has granted us a lovely convent by a lake. I could use your skill with my accounts. You may decide to take your vows with us."

The following Sunday, I joined Andreas and Aspasia for our usual meal by the sea. I told them about Empress Evdokia's demand and Princess Irini's dream. They burst out laughing.

"That Irini of Athens took a risk," Aspasia commented, spooning a sea urchin from its half-shell nestled in a bowl of seaweed. "The Abbess could have said that the devil sent the dream. The Empress would have called the Princess a heretic and got her exiled."

"No, no," Andreas shook his head. "Princess Irini's dream makes Co-emperor Leon look virile and manly. Princess Irini is safe until the Empress thinks up a better scheme to get rid of her."

"Why did Empress Evdokia not ask Doctor Moses if Princess Irini is with child?" I asked. "He is her physician."

"A physician is loyal to his patients," Andreas said. "Especially this one."

Aspasia lowered her voice. "What if she is not with child?"

He smiled. "She wouldn't lie about a condition that will be obvious very soon."

"And if she bears a daughter?"

"A son will come, eventually."

"Abbess Anthusa has invited me to make a retreat at her convent at Mantinia," I said.

They both stared at me in alarm. "She wants you to take the vows," said Aspasia.

Andreas looked horrified. "You won't, will you?"

"I don't want to be a nun," I said irritably. "I just need fresh air. I'm sick of stone walls and stinking pisspots thrown out windows."

Andreas walked me down the steps to Ta Gastria. He took my hands. "Don't go to Mantinia," he said. "Stay here. Marry me. Please say you will. I don't care that you were betrothed. I don't care that you can't find that bastard. I have a good job and a good future. We will live in the medical compound. Our children will grow up safe and healthy."

His handsome face was so earnest and his smile so sweet that my heart melted. He was offering me a golden future. So why was panic rising in my throat?

"I will go to Mantinia. When I return, we will marry."

He frowned. "Then I'll go with you. A woman cannot travel alone. Especially now. Armies are on the march. Caliph al-Mansur has attacked the sea fortress of Syke. The Emperor has sent cavalry units from three themes. Wait a month until this is over."

My temper flared. "I walked to Constantinople from Ikonion. I know how to travel safely. I'll join a caravan leaving from Chalkidon."

His face darkened. "You aren't going on retreat. You are dreaming of going back to village life, like when you were an innocent child and your spirit was bound by your family and your village. You can't go back. You are different now."

He was right about part of that. I wanted the comforting lanes of a village around me and the quiet stars. And who was to say whether I could go back or not?

Abbess Pulkeria also tried to change my mind. "Emperor Constantine has sent Commander Mihalis the Dragon to shut down monasteries and convents all over Bithynia. They are burning scrolls and codices written by the Church Fathers. They are selling off the monastery possessions and giving the money to Emperor Constantine. This is not the time to travel to a convent."

But I was determined. As summer approached, Abbess Pulkeria relented and said she would find me a suitable travelling companion. One morning, I passed

Elias on Mesi Street walking with other rich gentlemen. Our eyes met. I looked away. Even in Constantinople where women were freer than in towns and villages, a woman on her own could not speak to a man walking with other men. She would be thought a whore.

After a few minutes, he came hurrying up behind me. "I'm leaving Constantinople," I said abruptly. "I have given up looking for Myrizikos."

He steered me to a kapelarion and shouted for skewers of pork chunks sizzling on the grill and mugs of watered wine. I squeezed a lemon over the skewers and bit off a chunk. Delicious hot fat dripped down my chin.

"Why are you going home?" he demanded. "Wasn't your father going to marry you to the bone-scraper?"

"I'm going to the Convent of Abbess Anthusa at Mantinia."

"You're taking the vows?" He looked so horrified that I had to laugh.

My bad mood slipped away as it always did with him. "Abbess Anthusa has invited me to take retreat there. I need to get outside these walls and breathe clean air."

He listened intently to my story of my visit to the Palace with Abbess Anthusa. It felt good to be talking to him again.

"Is Irini of Athens really with child?" he demanded. "Did the Abbess say for sure?"

"The Abbess told me later that the Princess's dream kept her from having to obey the Empress's conniving. If the Abbess had predicted that the Princess was with child, and then a child never came, the Emperor would have punished Abbess Anthusa."

Elias shook his head. "The Emperor won't touch a hair of the Abbess's old head. He needs her. Mantinia is in the theme of Paphlagonia on the Pontus Sea. Across the Pontus lie the Bulgar Khanate and the Caliphate and the Magyars and the Goths. If they attack the harbours of Paphlagonia, they can reach the gates of Constantinople in only three days. Emperor Constantine needs the people of Paphlagonia to billet and feed the imperial army and navy. He needs to conscript their sons. Abbess Anthusa is revered in Paphlagonia. So, the Emperor funds her double monastery and looks the other way when she keeps painting icons and distributing them over the countryside. And in return, she tells the people that he is a good emperor."

He sat back and regarded me thoughtfully. "Why travel so far? Convents in Bithynia also have fresh air and silence."

"Abbess Anthusa said she needed help with her accounts."

"That's the only reason?"

I stared into my wine cup. "I've had an offer of marriage. The assistant to Doctor Moses. He doesn't care that I am betrothed. He would give me a comfortable life. I need to think about it."

He raised his eyebrows. "And for this you travel all the way to Paphlagonia? Shouldn't you be staying here and seeing enough of him so that you can make a good decision?"

I didn't answer.

He sighed. "A caravan is leaving for Paphlagonia next month from Chalkidon. I'll reserve you a seat in a carriage."

"That's very kind of you," I stammered, surprised. "But Abbess Pulkeria has arranged for me to travel with some nuns going all the way to Mantinia. We will leave after Emperor Constantine goes on campaign."

I walked home thinking about Elias, wondering why he was helping me. I hardly noticed the flags and banners decorating the streets from the Milion to the Golden Gate for the upcoming military campaign. The week before, a sword and shield had been mounted on Chalke Gate to announce the campaign. Emperor Constantine's personal banner had been hung beside them to show that the Emperor himself was leading the campaign. For weeks, we had seen him in the kapelaria eating with his commanders, Bardanes Tourkos, Mihalis Melissinos, and Mihalis the Dragon.

The day they marched out of the city, I stood with Abbess Pulkeria on Mesi Street to cheer them on their way. People waved from rooftops and windows. Priests and monks held up gold crosses, relics of saints, and banners with the names of their church or monastery. We knelt as the bishop passed carrying the golden cross embedded with the Holy and Life-Giving Splinter of the Holy Cross. The Emperor's Tagmata passed in full armour. Was Myrizikos under that helmet? I couldn't tell.

The Emperor and his commanders would sleep at his palace at Evdomon tonight and cross the Propontis by warship to Pendykion harbour in the morning. They would march to Malagina and join the theme armies. In a month or more, they would return with booty and prisoners. Or carrying the helmets of our dead.

I left Constantinople on the first Monday in June. It was a fine warm day. I was dressed for walking in a knee-length linen tunica, loose trousers, and sturdy new sandals. My satchel held a spare tunica, underclothes, shoes, and a letter from Abbess Pulkeria verifying my identity. This would get me a free bed in a convent dormitory. My remaining clothes, my writing table, and my glass necklace were safe in the convent storeroom.

Tears spilled from my eyes when I went to Abbess Pulkeria's study to say goodbye. I knelt to kiss the hem of her tunica. When I rose, there on her palm lay my tiny icon of Saint Thekla. She closed it between my hands. Joy and relief flooded me. Saint Thekla and I were together again.

Chapter XI

Dark foreboding dragged my feet as I passed under the gaze of the golden angels guarding the Golden Gate. I had not found Myrizikos. Instead I had found kind people and employment. I was giving those up just to smell green grass and see the horizon? This was madness. I started to turn around and beg Abbess Pulkeria to take me back.

"Cousin Thekla! Wait!" A shout shattered my dark mood. My heart gave a leap. A shabby monk in rough sandals hurried up and sketched a cross in the air. "Good day and power to us all, Sisters."

My companions glared at him and picked up their pace. Elias addressed me in a loud voice.

"Dear Cousin Thekla! Yesterday I received word that your mother is ill. I have come to accompany you home. It's a miracle that I found you."

"Why the monk outfit?" I muttered. "Are you spying for the Eparch of the Monasteries again? Or hiding from some creditor?"

"I am bringing God's holy word to the far reaches of the empire."

"Like your holy work at the brothel?" I snapped, irritated.

He raised his eyebrows. "Why so gloomy? You are going to visit a living saint."

"I'm making a mistake," I blurted. "My home is here. I should stay."

He sighed. "Women are such place-bound creatures. A man spends a night in a lodging and forgets it the next day. A woman calls it home. But how is your retreat a mistake? You will come back to Constantinople. You will marry and have many children. You will cook all day for the good doctor and his nurses and his patients. There will be no more lonely wandering through the shops and stopping to eat grilled shrimp with friends. Still, cheer up. You might meet a nice farm lad and marry him instead of your doctor's assistant. Then you'll have all the green grass that you want."

I had to laugh as I elbowed my way onto the loaded ferry. The sailors raised the sails, the summer wind caught us, and we shot along the sea walls where I used to sit gazing at the sea. Cold water drenched me. I clutched the railing, already seasick. Elias pulled a dirty cloth bundle from his knapsack and offered around squished pork buns. The nuns looked away. I reached for one, thinking the bread might settle my stomach. One sniff and the nausea got worse. I fixed my eyes on the shining

193

golden domes of the Churches of Holy Wisdom and Saint Irini. Only eight months ago when I arrived, the city had been a jumble of rooftops. Now I could name all the buildings.

No sooner had Elias directed my eyes up the Straits of Bosporus than we were slipping into the busy harbour of Chalkidon. Slaves were winching up huge marble slabs with tall cranes and swinging them onto cargo ships. White marble dust blanketed everything, quarried in the pale gashes in the hills above the town, where Elias pointed. The nuns headed towards the caravan of coaches and wagons loading up for Paphlagonia. They would follow along the Straits of Bosporus to the Pontus Sea and then along the coast of Paphlagonia. My heart lifted. I was eager to see this sea that I had heard was so broad that even a soaring eagle could not see across it. But Elias pulled me towards the markets.

"Let us buy our mid-day meal and then get on the road. We can make it to Pendykion by dusk. It's only twenty miles and the days are long."

I stopped walking. "Pendykion is the wrong way."

"Oh, didn't I mention? Slight detour. I have business in Pendykion. We'll take a short cut from there over the mountains. I have to meet a monk along the way. You'll stay in a nice convent, Saint Emmelia. The Pontus Sea is just beyond and we'll catch a boat to Mantinia. We will get there before this caravan. Of course you can join your companions in that caravan. It will leave in a few hours. Or tomorrow, maybe."

I looked at the caravan. Slaves were just starting to load the wagons. It would be hours before the caravan left, as I knew from experience in Amorion. I spoke to Elias sternly.

"At Pendykion, we go straight to Mantinia. No stops except this Saint Emmelia convent."

"Word of honour." He held up his hand.

"Such as it is," I muttered.

We bought cheese, dried apricots, and rusks. The sea sparkled blue; warm winds pushed us forward. A brief rest for lunch and we reached the heavy gates of Pendykion fortress at dusk. We had passed through here on the way to Constantinople. We had sat on the beach and eaten grilled fish. Elias had named the islands floating in the evening mist. This time, though, we went through the tunnel under the walls and I turned towards the convent.

Wait!" he called. "Extract a few folles from your heavy purse and pay for a bed at the pandohion. The mattresses are surely softer than at the convent. And the food will be far better."

The fragrance of grilled fish wafting from the kapelarion decided me. Supper at the convent would be thin lentil soup. I reached for my purse.

The windows in the women's dormitory at the pandohion overlooked the kapelarion garden. Elias was lounging on cushions at a low table, knocking back a mug of wine with a uniformed postal courier. I left my satchel on a bunk and went down to use the toilet and wash basin. Elias was alone when I got to the table. A waiter banged down a platter of grilled grouper mounded with fried artichokes and spring peas. The fresh fennel and dill fronds sprinkled over it tickled my nose. I pulled out my knife and spoon.

"Akepsimas would have high praise for this," I smiled as I dug in. I took a tentative taste of the wine that Elias had poured. "Rich but with a tangy bite," I judged. "Certainly better than the acidic rosé that Abbess Pulkeria serves."

Elias laughed. "Only last autumn, you didn't know the difference between wine and vinegar. Now you're an expert."

We wiped the platter clean with bread and ate the sweet, spongy fried dough balls drizzled with honey with a splash of lemon flower water. That night I slept well on a decent straw mattress, strengthening my body and spirit for our journey. We climbed flower-covered hills through grass so green it hurt the eyes. At mid-day, we lingered over our olives and cheese and napped in dappled shade. That night we slept in each other's arms outside a shepherd's hut while the shepherd snored and his great white dog watched over the goats and sheep. I smiled into the star-filled sky. How I had longed for this embrace, how joyful was my heart. I floated through the stars and fell asleep to the gentle goat bells and owls calling to their mates.

The next two nights we slept at the edge of a forest, then late the fourth day, we topped a hill. Before us stretched a blue sea so vast that the Propontis looked like a pond.

"The Pontus Sea," Elias waved. "Which we share with the Bulgars, the Magyars, the Goths, and the Caliph. And the Khazars, where Emperor Constantine's first wife was born."

A longing came over me to walk the rim of that vast

sea until I had seen all these lands, but we turned away again and dusk found us on a steep ridge overlooking a slender valley filling up with evening shadows. Two monasteries faced each other across fields, orchards, and a gentle stream.

"The double monasteries of Saint Emmelia, monks on that side, nuns over here. We will enjoy their hospitality for two nights while I chat with my friend. It's too late to bang on the gates now. The stars will be our blanket one last night."

The stream in the valley was a silver thread of moonlight when we finished the last of our cheese and olives. I stretched out on my cloak on the sweet grass and we lay in each other's arms. "I won't stay at the convent," I murmured. "I'll float here in the stars until you come back."

But morning came and he was gone. Gone were his satchel, walking stick, and cheerful grin. I stared, disbelieving, at the pressed-down grass where he had lain. I stood up and scanned the forest and the valley with increasing confusion. No solitary monk was down there greeting the monks who were coming out to the fields. I dropped to my knees and cried. I fumbled Saint Thekla out of my scarf and gazed into her sweet face.

"Is this my life, to be abandoned and humiliated by men?" I sobbed.

She didn't answer. After a while, I dried my tears and tied her back into my scarf. When I started down the hill, the sky had lost its blue and the flowers had no scent. The summer breeze was cold.

Groups of nuns were herding goats into the pastures. They welcomed me with smiles and directed me up the lane beside the orchard where yellow kitrons peeked between the leaves. The barns, paddocks, and stone walls of the convent were just beyond. Abbess Fanouria was a small sturdy nun with the weathered face and muscular hands of a farm woman. I knelt to kiss the hem of her worn linen tunica. She poured us both cool lemon water and we sat at the kitchen table while she read my letter from Abbess Pulkeria.

"My cousin and I are going on retreat at Mantinia," I explained. "He is staying at the monastery. He will come for me in two days." I forced myself to smile but my despairing heart was weeping. He wouldn't come, I knew. I would stay here until I found a travelling companion to continue with me on to Mantinia.

"Stay as long as you can," Abbess Fanouria smiled. "We need a calligrapher. A wealthy patron who takes retreat with us has lent us two scrolls—histories of women saints. I have prayed to have copies for our small library. You are the answer to my prayers. Perhaps you can teach my literate nuns how to copy."

I joined the nuns in the fields. At mid-day, we ate dried apricots, barley bread, and hard cheese washed down with clear stream water. At dusk, we washed in the stream and went into the little church for Esperinos prayers. I stared. All around me on the walls, ceiling, and pillars were painted images of saints, village scenes, and animals—in all the colours of God's creation. They seemed to move in the flickering tallow candlelight.

"The monks from the monastery painted these icons," smiled Abbess Fanouria with pride.

"Are you not afraid that Mihalis the Dragon will burn

you down?" I whispered.

She shook her head confidently. "Emperor Constantine allows Abbess Anthusa at Mantinia their icons. He will not deny us ours."

I untied Saint Thekla from my head scarf and held her between my hands during prayers. That night I placed her in the niche above my bed.

We rose to the scent of dawn and fell asleep to the calls of owls. We picked lemons and lowered them into the well to keep cool. We peeled and boiled the rinds in honey water to make spoon sweets. We collected pine cones and laid them to dry so we could crack them open and take out the pine kernels. In the winter, the nuns would eat them with plumped raisins and honey. We twice-boiled hyacinth bulbs and ate them with fresh sweet peas or fava beans. Some we preserved in vinegar. We gathered walnuts and made preserve and brandy. The cellar held their elderberry, lilac, fig, walnut, and rose petal wines. We made evkrata from the juice of early sour crab apples which we mixed with honey and wine. We made verjuice from unripe grapes.

The days stretched into weeks and the slow, quiet life drew me in. The nuns' quiet prayers floated over the fields as we weeded and hoed. The gentle tending of plants and animals soothed the confusion in my heart. I taught the two literate nuns how to prepare a parchment for writing and they began copying the donor's scrolls. I began to copy the story of Saint Emmelia who was mother to Saint Basil of Kaisaria, Saint Makrina, and Saint Gregor of Nyssa.

Abbess Fanouria's governing was milder than Abbess

Pulkeria but then she wasn't feeding and sheltering destitute women or satisfying the whim of an empress or placating wealthy women who gave paltry donations. Saint Emmelia convent was simply a place of peace.

Too peaceful, I sometimes thought, remembering my pleasure walking through the busy marketplaces of Constantinople. Still, I wondered if this might be the place for me—farm life with women who looked after each other. Elias was right, a woman's heart quickly finds a home. Saint Thekla had brought me here. Perhaps she meant for me to stay.

On Fridays after Ninth Hour prayers, while we ate thick lentil soup and heavy bread and drank water spiced with fennel, Abbess Fanouria read aloud from the typikon, the founding document for the convent. It listed the rules for living a harmonious and productive life. Then, on the fourth Sunday of my stay, Abbess Fanouria stopped me outside the church. "You have been with us for a month. Your cousin has not returned."

I continued tying Saint Thekla into my scarf, avoiding her eyes. "He must have decided to stay longer, Abbess."

"The abbot from the monastery will come today to chant our services. I will ask about your cousin."

The abbot never came.

Warhorses galloped out of the forest bearing soldiers waving blazing torches and whips. They thundered through the convent gates and into the church. We were trapped before we even knew to run. The screams of their warhorses joined our own. Smoke and flames filled the church. The tapestries went up like flaming pillars. The wooden icons on stands crackled like kindling. I heard the saints on the walls wailing in terror. I saw their white spirits rise to heaven. A kick knocked me to my knees. I looked up to a mounted soldier above me who raised his whip hand. Mihalis the Dragon had come, just as I had feared. His warhorse reared and I ran under its raised hooves out the door. Soldiers were whipping nuns down the lane. Smoke rose from the monastery.

I flung myself over the wall into the sheep pen and crawled under their milling bodies to the gate, then through the bars and across the corn field into the forest. Underbrush tore my clothes. I crawled under the blackberry brambles and pressed my hands over my mouth to stifle my sobs. Warhorse hooves crashed nearby.

"I'll go back for torches!" a soldier shouted. "We'll burn down the forest."

"No need. The convent and the monastery are burnt. That's all the Dragon wants."

All night, I lay on sharp blackberry thorns, clutching Saint Thekla to my heart, afraid to move, afraid to call out to any nuns hiding nearby in case soldiers might hear. At dawn, I crawled out. Nuns and monks were creeping from the forest. Black smoke rose from the convent and the monastery. Carrion crows and buzzards circled. The monks went back to their monastery. We went home.

They were hiding inside the barn, Mihalis the Dragon and his soldiers. They dragged us into the courtyard. The Abbess lay there, dead, her body trampled by warhorse hooves. Other nuns had died around her, their faces burnt and blackened. We buried them in the vegetable garden while the soldiers laughed. They roped us together and dragged us away. A line of monks was being dragged from the monastery. They tied us to them.

Five days they dragged us over the hills to Pendykion. The first night, I heard screaming. I pulled out my knife and cut through the rope that bound me. I crawled toward the screaming but I could not stop the violence against her body. A soldier grabbed my knife and threw himself on me. If I hadn't twisted his balls like my brothers had taught me, I too would have felt his violence. Two days later, we dug the abbot's grave with our hands.

"Did a monk called Elias come some weeks ago?" I whispered to the monk clawing the earth beside me. He shook his head. Relief flooded me. Elias was safe! Then came anger. Elias had worked for the Eparch of the Monasteries. He had gone back and reported the icons at the monastery and the convent. He had left me here to die. I would find him and slit his throat.

A flock of chattering sparrows flitted through some low sumac bushes, pecking at the bright berries. Were they sent by Saint Thekla? I wondered. Was she saying that I would survive?

On the fourth night, we reached Pendykion. All night we shivered on the beach. The dark shapes of the prison islands lay outlined against the stars. Elias had recited their names. All I could remember was Prinkypos Island, where Emperor Constantine had exiled the old Patriarch. Was Prinkypos Island also to be our fate?

A warship arrived. Weak from hunger and exhaustion, I crawled up the gangplank. I barely saw the people of Pendykion watching from the city walls. The warship turned towards the walls of Constantinople. The city where I had found a new life was to be the city of my death. We dropped anchor by the Golden Gate and soldiers pushed us into rowboats, then dumped us on the beach. They whipped us through the Golden Gate. The bars of a prison swung open and I tumbled into darkness.

We moistened our lips with water that seeped from the walls. We ate mouldy bread flung by jailors who taunted us with the humiliations and tortures that lay before us.

"You will be stripped naked and put backwards on a donkey. People will throw rocks at you and spit on you. You will be blinded, branded, beaten to death. You will be exiled to the lands of the pagans."

Death's cold fingers were slipping around me. I crawled to the bars for a last look at the sky. The jailors had left the outer prison door open. A breeze brought the scent of fried fish. A street urchin poked a stick at me.

"Go to the convent of Ta Gastria," I croaked. "Tell the novice at the gate that Thekla of Ikonion is here. You will get money." He said a filthy word. I held Saint Thekla in my hands. "Take me to Heaven, Saint Thekla. I can bear no more."

I was wakened by a rough shout that echoed through the dungeon. "On your knees, filthy scum. You're getting what's coming to you!"

A white light floated before me. Saint Thekla was so near that I could touch her silvery slippers. Her clear voice filled my ears.

"Jailor! Why are these clerics locked in here?"

"They is idol-worshippers. Caught cavorting with

icons. Commander Mihalis the Dragon burnt down their monasteries."

"Open the gate! Let them out."

"What?"

"You hear me, disgusting imbecile! I will have your throat cut. Guards! Bring these people out!"

Gates clanged. I lifted my icon over my head.

"Dear Saint Thekla," I said to the pillar of light. "Here is your icon. I have been faithful to you. Please take me with you to heaven."

Celestial hands lifted me. Holy water washed over me. Above me floated golden walls and golden angels with lifted wings. Saint Thekla was taking me to heaven.

Chapter XII

A small green island with two peaks, one crowned with a monastery. An island of two stremmata—what an ox can plough in two days. A small fishing harbour surrounded by cottages with red tiled roofs, vegetable gardens, and kitron trees heavy with fruit. Barley fields flowed up steep slopes to open pastureland where goats and sheep grazed and women harvested bitter greens. Oregano and thyme tossed their scents into the breeze and migrating birds feasted on red, orange and yellow sumac berries. Prinkypos Island.

There is a particular quiet that is dawn when the earth takes its first breath. I opened my eyes to the heavy aroma of millet porridge. I was wrapped in a blanket and lying on a wooden floor. Seabirds floated past a window to a pink sky. I struggled to sit up. An old woman brought me a bowl of porridge. My fingers were too weak to hold the spoon so she fed me with her hand. The sweet warmth cleared my head and I looked around. Five nuns from Saint Emmelia were sitting near me, eating from wooden bowls. I reached for the nun next to me. We clung to each other.

"Sister Matrona!" I sobbed, "Are we in heaven?"

"I only know we are alive."

A young man in a long faded tunica with his hair pulled into a bun like a priest came in the door and closed it carefully behind him. He stood, pulling nervously at his scraggly beard. He spoke in a low voice, tense with strain.

"Sisters, I am Father Dimitrios, the priest here on Prinkypos Island. This is my mother's cottage. An imperial vessel left you on the dock last night. The captain said you were from Dalmatiou Prison being transferred here to the prison monastery."

He wrung his big hands. "Sisters, I explained that the prison monastery is abandoned. There are no monks, no jailors. Everyone left when they took the old Patriarch away. The captain left you here anyway. He went on to Proti Island to leave off his other prisoners, he said. Monks."

"We are in prison?" I quavered, confused.

"No, no." Father Dimitrios pulled at his sparse beard. "There used to be a prison monastery here. It was abandoned two years ago. There are no jailors. No prisoners."

"So we are free?" I couldn't understand.

He shook his head sadly, "You are still prisoners of the Emperor. The captain will return with new orders. He will take you to another prison. All these islands have prisons. You must leave before he comes back. Our fishermen will take you across the Propontis to Bithynia.

There are convents that will take you in. The big monasteries are all paired with convents."

I looked at the nuns, bewildered. They too looked confused and frightened.

The priest's young voice trembled. "Listen to me, Sisters. I was the priest for the old Patriarch. I fed him when he was ill. I heard his confession. When they took him to Constantinople, I went with him. I stood by him when they stripped him and put him backwards on a donkey. I wiped the blood from his body when people threw stones at him. I knelt with him in the Hippodrome while the new Patriarch Nikitas read off the anathemas. For every anathema, the old patriarch received a lash. I heard his last confession. I witnessed the executioner lift his sword."

He lifted his clasped hands. "Escape now, I beg you, Sisters. The ghost of the old patriarch roams the monastery. Do not make me also see yours."

Confusion flooded me. Saint Thekla had saved me from death and brought me to this sanctuary. Now I had to leave? I fumbled for her in the corner of my scarf. But the scarf that wrapped my throat was not mine and neither was the tunica I was wearing. I clutched the old woman who was feeding me the porridge.

"Where are my clothes, Auntie?"

"We had to burn them, dear heart. They were filthy rags."

She raised the spoon to my lips but dismay and despair flooded me. I turned my face away. I had not protected Saint Thekla. I had let her burn.

Early the next morning, Sister Matrona and the other

four nuns climbed into a fishing boat to escape to Bithynia. But a strange weakness had taken over my legs. I could not rise from the chair. Father Dimitrios knelt by me.

"It is time to leave, Sister Thekla. Everyone is waiting for you."

"Tell them to go without me," I whispered. I closed my eyes.

"Why do you not save yourself?"

I forced the words from my lips. "When our village priest baptised me, he put in my hands a tiny icon of Saint Thekla of Ikonion. I have carried her since I was a child. She has protected me and I have protected her. But I have let her burn. Now she cannot protect me. The soldiers will find me no matter where I am."

Father Dimitrios took my hands. "My child, Saint Thekla is not just the bit of wood that you have carried. Yes, wherever is the saint's image, so is the saint. But Saint Thekla is everywhere. She brought you here. If you are too weak to stand, that is because she wants you to stay—but to live, not to die. If soldiers come, we will protect you."

So I remained on Prinkypos Island. Guilt and despair were my jailors. The screams of the nuns at Saint Emmelia convent filled my ears. My eyes saw the nuns that we had buried. The priest's widowed mother spoke but her voice came from far away. Her porridge had no taste or smell. The sky held no blue.

Each day, Father Dimitrios helped me to a bench outside his mother's door. He sat beside me and told me the names of the villagers as they passed. He named their children and goats and sheep and donkeys. He placed flowers in my unfeeling hands. He sat me on a boulder on the beach with my unfeeling feet in the water. He pointed at the sea birds and named the white kataraktes and the dark alkyoni diving for fish. But my eyes couldn't see them.

Then one morning, why I do not know, I awoke to the singing of wind through the masts of the fishing boats. I smelled wood smoke and the fragrance of baking bread. I went outside and the earth was warm under my bare feet. I knelt in the garden and smelled mint and oregano. Church bells were ringing. The widow took me to celebrate the fifteenth of August, the day of the Assumption of the Mother of God into Heaven.

"Welcome to the living," Father Dimitrios smiled. We sat in the plateia for the feast celebrating the holy day. He handed me a knife so I could eat, and a sheath on a belt. "We were afraid to give you this before but now we know you are well."

Some days later, I walked the length of the village. A path drew me into a pine forest and up a steep hill. Cool breezes brought the scent of the sea. A fancy yacht was passing, its oars flashing in the sun. I had seen similar yachts swooping in and out of the harbours of Constantinople. The yacht rounded the corner of the island and went out of sight. My eyes moved to the other islands in the chain and beyond them to the mountains of Bithynia. Memories formed—Elias walking beside me up a flower-drenched hill, the sky above us flashing with stars, the Church of Saint Emmelia and its icon-covered walls. I fell to my knees and my tears poured into the earth. I wept until I was empty. I sat for a while, feeling strangely calm and strong. I got to my feet and continued up the path.

At the top of the path was a high stone wall with a locked wooden gate—the monastery where Patriarch Constantine had lived his last years. I followed the outside of the walls until I came upon a fig tree that had broken through the wall. A need came over me to be sheltered within the arms of a convent. I climbed up the twisted branches and over the wall.

I was in a vegetable garden choked with weeds. Vines heavy with grapes covered a trellis. Beyond was a sizeable orchard, carefully pruned. The villagers were tending the trees. I could see apples, pears, kumquats, apricots, and quince. A pomegranate tree spread its ripening fruit over the wall near a persimmon tree.

Near a door sat a covered open shed with a brick oven and an iron kettle hanging on a cross-bar over the charred remains of a fire. I pushed open the door into a kitchen. A stone sink drained under a window into the garden. Three broken chairs sat around a large wooden table. The next room had two long slate tables and many benches. The refectory. This monastery had housed a lot of monks.

The refectory opened into a hall with more doors, probably offices and storerooms for the monks' seasonal clothing and supplies. One door opened into a room with a low corner fireplace and a wooden couch pulled near it. The only other furniture was a small desk and chair. The abbot's study. The poor Patriarch had burnt the furniture to stay warm.

I opened the long double windows that reached the ground and pushed open the shutters. I stepped out into a sunny courtyard with a small church in the centre. Around it were the work rooms of the monastery with the dormitories on the upper level, like at Saint Emmelia convent. I pictured the monks busy at carpentry and leather working, weaving, perhaps copying scrolls in a scriptorium. The wing that connected the long wings of the monastery had wide double doors, probably the entrance facing the main gate. This had been a sizeable and wealthy monastery.

My need for the comfort of a convent's shelter was gone. I went back through the abbot's study windows and closed them behind me. As I went into the hall, I saw stone steps leading up to the dormitory level. I could get a swallow's eye view of the compound. At the top stretched a long dark hall with doors on both sides. I opened the first door and swung open the shutters. Below me lay the vegetable garden and the fig tree. Mice had chewed through the leather straps of the wooden bed frame. I crossed to the cell opposite and threw open the shutters.

Instantly came a shout, "Someone is up there! Guards!"

I froze. Below me, a group of men and women were staring up at me. I saw Father Dimitrios. They must have come from the fancy yacht I had seen earlier. They had come up the lane and he must have opened the gate for them when I was exploring the convent. Terrified, I ran down the steps but the guards caught me at the bottom. They dragged me to the courtyard and threw me onto the stones.

A familiar voice pierced my terror. "Thekla! Mama, it's Thekla from Ta Gastria Convent!"

Another familiar voice let out a shocked shriek. "Megalo! Get away from that filthy peasant!"

Father Dimitrios's voice came then. I felt his arm over me. "Thekla is my cousin. She lives here."

To my astonishment came Princess Anthusa's familiar whine. "Release her, guards."

And another voice, clear and light. "You know this peasant, Anthusa?"

"Indeed I do," said Anthusa. "And so should you, dear sister-in-law. She was Abbess Anthusa's companion the day you described your so interesting dream."

"Let her go." The lighter voice held real authority.

Father Dimitrios helped me to my feet. I looked at the people staring at me. There was little Megalo, looking frightened, and Patrikia Constanta. Her expression of horror was matched by Doti and Tisti who were clinging to each other. Beside them stood Princess Irini. She looked me over, then turned to Father Dimitrios.

"I am too warm, Father. I wish to sit down and rest. Somewhere cool and quiet."

"The abbot's study." He led the guards over to a door.

Megalo scuttled over to me and took my arm. "How did you get here?" she whispered.

I felt stronger next to her familiar presence. I brushed the dust off my tunica. "Long story," I whispered.

Father Dimitrios and the guards had opened the long windows of the abbot's study and were looking at us. "The room is safe to enter, Highness," the guard called.

Princess Irini went over to the long windows. She held out her hand and the guard helped her over the sill. She said something to Father Dimitrios. The priest hurried over to me.

"Sister Thekla, the princess wishes to speak to you," he said with a worried frown.

Dumbfounded, I started towards the open window. Princess Anthusa sidled up to me. "Whatever Irini tells you, you will tell me," she hissed. "Or I will tell my father that you have an icon. You will go back to Dalmatiou Prison and never get out."

I gaped at her. "How did you know I was in Dalmatiou Prison?"

Her thin lips curved in a sly smile and she moved away. I went over to the study.

Princess Irini was sitting on a chair behind the desk with her legs propped up on a chair someone had brought from the kitchen. She had taken off her sandals and her feet were so swollen that her sandal straps had cut into them. I dropped to my knees and put my forehead on the floor.

"Get up." Her voice was low and intense. She glanced out the long windows. The others were moving to the shade of the church. She turned her huge dark eyes on me. "You were in Dalmatiou Prison. Kneeling on the steps. Weren't you? Don't lie."

I stared at her. The intensity of her voice confused me.

"Answer me!"

"Yes, Princess," I stammered.

"You pushed an object into my hand."

"An object? What do you mean?" I stammered.

"A bit of wood. Painted with the figure of a woman. You pushed it into my hand."

"Saint Thekla! Oh thank the saints and angels! She didn't burn!" I put my hands over my mouth but I couldn't stop my sobs of relief and joy.

"An icon," she said with satisfaction. "I thought as much. I have only seen one and that was years ago. Anthusa bribed you to push it into my hand, didn't she?"

"Anthusa? What do you mean?" My joy mingled with confusion.

"Anthusa knows you from Ta Gastria convent. She got the icon from there. Or from some other convent that she frequents. Anthusa told you to push it into my hand."

I was horrified. "No, no! Abbess Pulkeria never gave her my icon. She gave it back to me. I had my icon in prison. I gave her to Saint Thekla when she came to take me to heaven."

She glanced out the window. "You put it in my hand. But I hid it before Anthusa saw it. Otherwise Anthusa would have told the guards and got me arrested." Her eyes were following the women now going into the church. "Evdokia's spies search my closets every day. If they ever find an icon, Leon will divorce me and exile me to that prison convent on Lesbos everyone whispers about. Evdokia's spies are out there now, my so-called Friends." She turned those dark eyes on me. "Did Anthusa threaten to have your tongue slit? That's her favourite threat."

It was coming to me now, the white light, the clear voice. I could barely babble out the explanation. "Princess, you were standing in the light. You were all white.

I thought you were Saint Thekla taking me to heaven. I gave you my icon to show I had been faithful."

She watched me like a hawk watches its prey. Then she smiled that dazzling smile that made the crowds shout her name. "Me? A saint? Oh, why not? Our Roman ancestors called their dead emperors gods, no matter how evil they were. Tell me, who is this Saint Thekla?"

"Saint Thekla of Ikonion First Woman Martyr and Equal to the Apostles. Patron saint of Ikonion. My name saint." I was babbling but I couldn't stop myself. Relief that I had not let Saint Thekla burn was making me giddy. It was all I could do not to laugh aloud.

Princess Irini was staring at me intently. "Does your saint perform miracles? I need a miracle to survive that godforsaken Palace. Evdokia is poisoning me. I throw up every morning."

"All pregnant women throw up." I blurted.

The smile vanished. "How did you know I was with child? My belly is not big."

"Your swollen feet, Highness," I stammered. "And I was with Abbess Anthusa when you told that story about your dream. You said that a saint came to you and told you that you carried in your womb a son of the Isaurians."

She laughed out loud. Heads turned outside. She lowered her voice. "That dream, what a joke. But the little Abbess believed me! Evdokia couldn't send me to that prison convent on Lesbos." She looked at her swollen feet and wriggled her toes.

"Doctor Moses promises that my feet will be normal after the baby comes. He tells me to prop them up." She turned that piercing gaze on me. "What was Anthusa telling you out there?"

Her abrupt change of subject startled me. "She said I had to tell her whatever you said or she would tell the Emperor that I have an icon."

Her eyes narrowed. "You have another icon?"

"No, no! She means Saint Thekla. She saw Saint Thekla at Ta Gastria. She wanted her. I refused."

"Courageous of you, but foolish. Anthusa doesn't like to be denied anything. Even my cousins in Athens were not as spoiled. Will you tell her what I say?"

"Never. I will never tell Princess Anthusa anything. Not ever. Nothing."

The anger that shook my voice satisfied her. She shifted her gaze to the people chatting or dozing in the shade of the church. As quick as the pickpockets in the Forum of Constantine, she slipped an object from her pocket and closed it inside the desk drawer.

"Take it back. It's yours. This will be our little secret. I had planned to throw it in the sea today but someone was always with me. I had to get it out of my closet before Evdokia's spies found it."

I covered my mouth to hold back my sobs. Princess Irini was watching the people outside.

"They are sulking because Empress Evdokia didn't take them to the mineral baths at Proussa. Evdokia took dozens of attendants and servants. She'll be there for weeks. She never takes me. I make her look uglier than she is. Emperor Constantine went with her. The baths ease the rash on his arms and legs. I saw it on the warship when we were coming from Athens. Sometimes the itching nearly drives him mad. I told him that the doctors in Athens call that kanker. They treat it with a poultice of grape hyacinth bulbs. In the spring, Theo and I went to the forests outside the Golden Gate and gathered some. I made the poultice and gave it to the Emperor. His doctors said hyacinths couldn't harm him, so they put it on his skin. The Emperor said it stopped the itching."

She sighed. "Now that I'm with child, the doctors won't let me get on a horse, or even sit on a beach. My poor cousin Theo is bored out of his mind. He goes shopping with me and the Chorus just to get out of the Palace."

"Chorus?"

"My so-called Friends, Doti and Tisti and Megalo. They are supposed to teach me Palace protocol. So many rules! Do nuns have such rules?"

I was taken aback. The princess thought I was a nun. I was afraid to correct her. "Monasteries and convents have a typikon. It lists the rules for living together, like tasks and duties and punishments and prayers for that day and the fasts."

"How do you remember all that?"

"The abbess reads it aloud at meals." I thought of Abbess Fanouria at Saint Emmelia convent lovingly reading the typikon. Sorrow made my throat ache. Princess Irini scowled.

"I would prefer that than listening to the gossip at the boring banquets I am forced to attend. I am beginning to agree with Anthusa about banquets."

She looked out the window. "My so-called Friends glance at each other when I do or say anything. They run to tell Empress Evdokia when they leave the Palace in the evening. When they are with me, they are useless. Doti kneels half the day in my private chapel and prays for me. Or she prays for a convent to accept her for a low entrance fee. Her son is marrying that child, Megalo. He will move in with his in-laws and Doti will have to live with them, which she doesn't want. And neither do they. The other Friend, Tisti, took a vow of celibacy after her fifth child, along with her husband, she believes. 'A celibate man in a city with a thousand prostitutes?' I said to her. Now she prays for me, too. Thank God they go home at dusk and leave me in peace with my slave and my eunuch, Iakovos."

"Can't you send them away?" I was feeling strong now that Saint Thekla was safe. I felt sorry for Princess Irini, trapped among people she hated.

"Evdokia appointed them. Only she can send them away. They gossip about everyone—who is important, who sits closest to the Emperor. There is a map of prestige in Constantinople and I don't have it. They made fun of my clothes until I begged the Emperor to have the Palace tailors sew me new ones. Then they sniggered because I had to beg. They mock my Athens accent and laugh at my provincial expressions." She scowled. "When I am empress, I will have all them exiled."

"You have no real friends?" The loneliness in her voice made my heart ache.

"Only Theo, my cousin. He lives in an adjoining suite to mine in Daphne Palace. My uncle sent him here to protect me. As if he could." She went silent, taken over by a strange sort of darkness.

"I am awakened by my slave and my eunuch. I pray in my chapel. When I am having breakfast, the Chorus arrives with the Palace head eunuch. He tells them my duties of the day. The Chorus decides what clothes I will wear. Then Theo comes for a few hours until I have to go to Empress Evdokia's apartments for my mid-day meal. He can't come. It's all women. The Empress sits like a giant toad and stuffs in sweets. Women come asking for favours. For this Evdokia takes money. One day, I will grant favours and have money and power over people. The Emperor gives Empress Evdokia whatever she wants because she gives him sons. What fortitude the Emperor has, to press his seed into that mountain of fat. No wonder he seeks his pleasure elsewhere."

I burst out laughing. So did she. She stretched out her swollen legs. "I stave off boredom by going to the Emperor's throne room in Magnavra Palace. Sister Thekla, you cannot imagine all the different kinds of people. They come from all over the world—strange skin colours, bizarre clothing, odd languages. They bring him gifts. He reads tax revenue reports. He reads postal dispatches. He signs documents. My husband just watches."

"The Emperor doesn't mind that you are there?"

"My husband minded. He told me I couldn't come there. So I wrote the Emperor a letter. I said that the mother of the heir to the throne should know how to educate her son. My eunuch Iakovos took the letter to the Emperor's household eunuch and persuaded him somehow to give it to the Emperor. Eunuchs run the Palace."

She rose stiffly and paced the room like a caged fox.

"My husband is an imbecile. He was betrothed to the daughter of King Pepin of the Franks and he still wants to be king of the Franks. He coughs all the time. Tuberculosis, his doctors say. I told them, 'Cure him.' They make excuses."

She gazed out the window. "I like this island. It's quiet here and smells of the sea. In Athens, my friends and cousins and I used to walk down the Sacred Way and swim in the sea at Elefsina. The ancients believed the god of the Underworld kidnapped Persephone there. Her mother, the goddess Demeter, turned summer into winter with her grief."

The homesick longing in her voice stirred in me a longing for the sweet-scented mornings of Anatolia, when I stepped outside into perfumed dew sparkling the grass and birds singing twig and branch. "Princess, you are not alone in your suffering. People used to laugh at my Anatolia accent and my crude manners and. . ."

"How could a peasant understand what I must endure!" Heads turned. The guards lunged towards the long windows. Princess Irini held up her hand. She dropped her voice to a whisper.

"Sister Thekla, I fear the devil has taken over my thoughts. I have become obsessed that my cousin Theo is poisoning me so that I will die and he can go home to Athens. See him there, the tall man in the green tunica? Does he seem possessed? You are a nun and familiar with good and evil."

But my eyes fell on the eunuch standing behind Theo. The sly expression on his smooth round face reminded me of the assistant cook in Amorion whose sly words bred distrust until he was sacked. The eunuch saw us looking and he hurried over to the long windows.

"Can I get Your Grace anything?" he asked with a smarmy smile.

"Water, Aetios. You are so helpful. I have a pressure in my chest. I cannot breathe."

Doti came near, waving a lace fan at her sweating face. "Highness, I have just been informed that the ghost of Patriarch Constantine haunts this island. What a terrible place for an outing! Why ever did your cousin suggest this grisly island?"

Theo had come over. He put his back to Doti and moved her aside. His eyes were on Aetios who was filling a tin cup with water from the goat skins the slaves had piled in the shade. "How did that eunuch get on your personal staff? He is a sneaky devil, always prying into everyone's affairs," he muttered.

"He brought a letter of introduction from some army commander."

"I am sure he wrote it himself."

Aetios returned with the cup. "Highness, the water smells odd. Make that nun taste this before you drink." He glanced at me.

"Throw it away," she said. "Once at Elefsina, we all became sick from water in a goatskin. You remember, Theo, we swam in the sea and ate pears under the olive trees. Doesn't this peaceful island remind you of Elefsina? I want to stay here. I cannot tolerate Constantinople another day. The stench in the streets! I cannot breathe." Tears filled her eyes.

Aetios edged closer. "Perhaps the Emperor will appoint you patroness of this monastery, Your Grace. It's an imperial monastery. You could come here whenever you please. Empress Evdokia sponsors imperial convents and goes there on retreat."

"Is that so?" Her face brightened. She called to Princess Anthusa who was sitting on the church steps. "Anthusa! What convents does your esteemed mother sponsor?"

"Mantinia, Ta Gastria, others. I don't remember." She didn't turn her head.

"Ta Gastria! That's why the Abbess lets you stay there whenever you wish."

"Those are convents," Doti inserted aggressively. "This is a monastery. You can't stay in a monastery."

"The Emperor can order the local bishop to reconsecrate it as a convent," countered Aetios smoothly. "The Chora was one of the oldest monasteries in Constantinople. Emperor Constantine revoked their charter and turned it into a prison. He took the Studios Monastery into imperial holdings. He can do what he wants."

"But the ghost of Patriarch Constantine haunts the place!" Doti shrilled.

"And many other ghosts, I wager," Theo teased. "This place has been a prison for a hundred years."

Doti crossed herself vigorously. "We must leave immediately, Highness. These ghosts will enter our bodies and take our souls!"

Theo pointed at Father Dimitrios. The priest was standing in a feeble strip of shade at the far side of the courtyard. "Have the village priest exorcise these poor ghosts. He must have experience warning off mermaids and sea nymphs."

Princess Irini laughed. "Bring him over here."

Theo beckoned and Father Dimitrios hurried over, his big fisherman's hands clasped to his chest. Princess Irini smiled at him. "Your name, Father?"

"Father Dimitrios, Highness."

"Father Dimitrios, I have heard that the ghost of Patriarch Constantine roams this monastery. Have you seen him?"

"Perhaps, Highness," he answered cautiously.

"I want you to exorcise him. And any other hovering spirits. Send them away. Now. Today. I want this monastery to be reconsecrated as a convent. I want to retire here to escape the Palace. How can I sleep if restless ghosts are drifting through my rooms?"

Father Dimitrios went pale. "Princess, I am a simple village priest. I have never performed an exorcism. Our bishop should do this. Particularly since it involves the ghost of a patriarch."

"The bishop is not here now. You are."

Father Dimitrios wrung his hands. "But Princess, what if the ghost won't leave?"

"God will send you the right words to make them leave."

"Begging your pardon but I was the Patriarch's priest. I went with him to Constantinople. I saw. . I. . . ."

Princess Irini frowned. Her voice grew stern. "Since you knew the Patriarch personally, his ghost will surely heed your command. Bring your incense and holy verses. As the old saying goes, 'Baptise and anoint whether he live or die.' We will have our lunch in the shade

223

while you assemble your paraphernalia." She changed her frown to a smile so sweet that his face went scarlet.

Poor young Father Dimitrios. My heart ached for him. He hurried across the courtyard, sandals flapping on the flagstones, his big shoulders hunched in the dull priest's tunica, crossing himself over and over.

Servants spread out food under the fruit trees in the shady orchard. I slipped into the kitchen. A noise made me whirl—a mouse skittering into a hole. I crossed my pounding heart. Father Dimitrios said he had seen the ghost of the Patriarch. Would the ghost enter my body and take my soul, as Doti had warned? I hurried to the abbot's study and eased open the desk drawer. Saint Thekla was truly there! My trembling fingers clasped her to my heart. I sat down and let her peace flow over me and into me.

Footsteps jerked me to my feet. I slid Saint Thekla back in the drawer. I would come back for her after they had all gone. Princess Anthusa had threatened to tell her father I had an icon. I couldn't risk carrying Saint Thekla with me until she had left. A figure crossed the long windows. Theo stepped inside. I put my hand on my knife.

He put on a charming smile. "I'm Theo, Irini's cousin from Athens. I hear you are Sister Thekla of Ta Gastria convent. Who were you before Ta Gastria?"

"Thekla of Ikonion."

"What did my cousin say to you so long in private?"

"Ask your cousin." I edged towards the door.

He stepped in front of me. "I will indeed. We have no secrets between us. You have no reason to trust me, of course. Ask me a question. If you believe my answer is honest, then answer mine."

I said the first thing that came to mind. "What is a Chorus?"

He laughed. "She told you about them? She must trust you. The Chorus are actors in a play. They comment on what is happening. Do you know what I'm talking about?"

"No."

"Let's just say that Irini's three attendants, her so-called Friends, comment on what Irini does, to her face and even more behind her back. I call them the Moirai, the Fates. Our Greek ancestors believed that three old women weave our destiny. Lachesis measures out the thread, Clotho spins it, and Atropos clips it when our life is over. I call Irini's Friends 'the Moirai' because they spin tales about her. One day I fear that their tales will clip the thread of her life."

His words chilled my heart. "She laughs at them."

"My cousin fears no one. She is suspicious and wary, but without fear. She was an orphan brought into an unwelcome household. Her courage raised her. When she was small, she believed that her parents had been captured by pirates. I cannot count the times we fetched her back from the port of Piraeus. She was trying to get onto a ship to free her parents from the pirates." He produced that charming smile. "Satisfied with my answer?"

I nodded.

"Now tell me. What did you and my cousin talk about all that time?"

"I think you should ask your cousin."

I heard Princess Irini's light voice calling his name. I stayed in the study until I heard his footsteps cross the courtyard. Then I went back outside to wait for Father Dimitrios.

Father Dimitrios returned, followed by all the villagers chattering with excitement and pride that one of their sons was going to banish a lingering ghost. I didn't care whether the ghost left or stayed. My thoughts were on Saint Thekla safe in the abbot's desk drawer. Had Saint Thekla made me give her to Irini of Athens to help her in some way? Had Saint Thekla made her return the icon to me? The thoughts made me dizzy.

Father Dimitrios stood on the steps of the little church in the centre of the courtyard and lit his incense ball. He swung it behind him and to both sides. At first, his voice trembled as he chanted the holy words that would release the ghosts of Patriarch Constantine and the others who had died here in exile. But as his chanting echoed against the monastery buildings, it seemed to me that unseen voices were chanting with him. Perhaps he heard them too, because his voice gained confidence. With real energy, he wafted holy smoke into the open doors of the little church and into the workshops. We followed him into the main building, coughing as he swung smoke into the refectory and kitchen, and up to the sleeping cells, and outside to the orchard and weed-choked vegetable garden. Scented smoke drifted into the water cisterns and latrines and the tumbled down goat shed and chicken house. A few of us followed him into the root cellar but Father Dimitrios alone went down to the rusted-shut doors of the dungeon.

As his voice floated over us, a sorrow that had pressed upon my heart lifted. A cool drop of rain spattered my cheek, but when I looked up into the blue summer sky, there wasn't a single cloud.

The sun was red and sinking into the sea when Father Dimitrios fell silent. We were all tired and caught up in our own thoughts. The village people hurried down the path. They had animals to feed. The imperial party straggled down in groups. Princess Irini beckoned me to walk beside her.

"You talked to my cousin Theo. What did he say?" she demanded.

"He told me about the Moirai, Highness."

Her tense face relaxed. "Ah, my so-called Friends. I don't worry about them. The Erinyes, the Furies, will take revenge on them if they harm me."

"Erinyes, Highness?"

"Women from the hips up and birds below, say our Greek ancestors. The Erinyes punished those who swore a false oath or did an evil act."

"They truly exist, these strange creatures?" I was astounded. The Chorus, the Morae, now the Erinyes? What next?

"The ancient playwrights wrote about them. Their eyes may have seen what ours cannot. When I was a child, I used to walk up to the Temple of Athena to watch the sunset. I could feel shapes flying around me. I thought they were the Erinyes."

A strange thrill went through me. "Where do they live, these half-women?"

"At Delphi, some say. In the caves behind the Asklepion, the healing centre. Women called Oracles used to sit in the Temple of Apollo below the Asklepion and predict men's fates. Perhaps the Erinyes were telling them what to say."

She moved ahead and I walked with Father Dimitrios. His feet dragged with fatigue.

"Do you still feel the ghost of the Patriarch, Father?"

His sigh held relief. "No, the poor man's soul is finally free. Before the Council at Hieria, he had preached the sanctity of icons. He changed his words when Emperor Constantine demanded that he persuade the Council to ban icons. I believe that betraying his beliefs weighed his soul down so that it could not rise to heaven. Now it has."

"Did he conspire against the Emperor, as he was accused?"

"He claimed his innocence to his dying breath."

At the bottom of the path, a shadow lunged out from the dark pines—Princess Anthusa. Father Dimitrios scurried ahead.

"What did Irini tell you?" Princess Anthusa hissed.

"Ask her." I moved on.

She snapped at my heels like a sheepdog. "You owe me your life, Thekla of Ikonion. I was at Ta Gastria when that beggar came around saying you were in prison. I got you out."

I stopped, surprised. "Why did you bother?"

"I didn't, actually. I went back to the Palace. Irini was prancing around in new clothes and praising my father's generosity. I said, 'Go look at his generosity at Dalmatiou Prison.' She was bored, so she went."

"She ordered the jailors to let us out. I heard her."

"Not because she cared. She just likes ordering people around. Her eunuch, Aetios, told her she couldn't revoke the Emperor's order. So she told the guards to transfer you somewhere, she didn't care where. Now tell me, what is Irini plotting? My mother has to know."

I tossed the words over my shoulder. "She talked about swimming in the sea."

Chapter XIII

Not for a minute did I believe that Emperor Constantine would reconsecrate the monastery as a convent. I laughed when the village people insisted that he would name Irini of Athens as sponsor. Empress Evdokia would block it. I had seen how devious the empress could be. She wouldn't let Princess Irini sponsor a convent and thus be equal to her. Still, I wished the princess all success. She had got me out of prison and had given me back Saint Thekla. For that, she had my loyalty.

Father Dimitrios had faith in her. The young priest stood taller after the exorcism. His shoulders were broader. He was so certain that Princess Irini would return as sponsor that he marked the day that she had come to Prinkypos in his Saint's Eortologion, as if Irini were another saint to remember in our daily prayers.

Three weeks passed by in Father Dimitrios's calendar of saints' days. Then, to my surprise, the imperial yacht slid into our small harbour and Princess Irini bounded down the gangplank with a smile as wide as the Pontus Sea. A group of serious men marched down behind her. They bowed their heads respectfully to Father Dimitrios and followed her into the Church of Saint Nikolaos to thank the saint for their safe voyage. There, Princess Irini stood at the front of the church, hands clasped piously, gazing at our simple wooden altar until the church was jammed with all of us. She prayed loudly so that everyone could hear.

"Dear Saint Nikolaos, thank you for bringing us safely to this beautiful island. May all the island's inhabitants have their nets filled with fish and their goats be fertile."

Minutes later, she was stepping up prettily on a tree stump in the plateia, one jewelled hand resting lightly on the shoulder of Father Dimitrios who looked like he was going to faint, the other hand lightly on her belly where the heir to the throne waited to be born. She took all of us captive with her words.

"Esteemed Roman citizens of Prinkypos. My heart overflows with gratitude for your kind welcome! What a beautiful island! No wonder there are such lovely people here! I am bringing good news. Thanks be to God, Emperor Constantine will reconsecrate the monastery as a convent. He has named me, the consort of Co-emperor Leon, as sponsor. Emperor Constantine has sent the imperial architects and Master Builders today. They will inspect the monastery. Please be so kind as to show them anything that needs repair. One day, your sisters and daughters will take their vows here and serve God in labour and in prayer."

How easily she commanded a crowd. How quickly we fell under her spell, so straight were her shoulders, so radiant her smile. She already wore the crown of an empress. Up the hill she marched, chatting happily to Father Dimitrios. Behind her panted the imperial architects and the Master Builder. Patrikia Constanta lagged behind with the three Friends and their sons, Theodore and Fanis. I heard Theo praising Father Dimitrios's widowed mother on her vegetable garden. What a charmer!

Princess Anthusa hung back by me, her plain features cold with contempt. "Irini of Athens is lying again. My father never said he would reconsecrate this dump as a convent. He never named her sponsor. The imperial architect and Master Builders are here only to estimate the cost of restoring it as a prison monastery."

"Why are you telling me this?" I refused to believe her. I kept my voice even.

"So you can tell the other peasants not to believe a word that liar says."

At that moment, my heart knew for certain that the monastery would indeed be a reconsecrated as a convent. My certainty grew stronger as I listened to the stonemason and the carpenter point out needed repairs. The Master Builder and architects dropped stones into the rainwater cisterns and the latrines. They climbed on the roofs and examined the chimneys. Princess Irini asked questions. Her cousin Theo stayed at her heels like a guard dog.

The August sun was a red ball sizzling into the sea when they finished. Princess Irini beckoned to me as we all stumbled down the lane, tired. She spoke quietly with her face turned towards me so no one else could hear.

"The Master Builder told me that the monastery can be made habitable with only a few repairs. I will need someone here on the island to watch their progress. I am naming you. You will be the haristikaris. Soon a bishop will come and reconsecrate it as a convent. Then repair work will begin. You will send me reports."

Shock stopped my breath. "What do you mean, send you reports?"

"Write me letters," she snapped. "I can't be here all the time, can I? I don't trust the builders. You will watch what they do and write me reports. You will send them by imperial post. Surely, there is a postal courier that comes to these islands. Get permission from your abbess at whatever convent you are from. You will live here on the island until the work is completed. Then you will remain here as abbess."

"Abbess?" I whispered. My lips went numb. My thoughts whirled. I couldn't stay on this island. I was going to marry Andreas. I was going to live in Doctor Moses's compound. I would be wife, mother, housekeeper, and cook.

"Of course, abbess," she snapped. "You will know everything about the convent. You know the village people. They like you. They will send their daughters to be nuns."

Except that I wasn't a nun. And I couldn't tell the princess this. She had assumed I was and I had not corrected her. She would accuse me of lying to her. I would die in prison.

"I can't be haristikaris, Princess," I babbled. "Or abbess. I have not lived in a convent long enough to know how to manage one."

"You are devout. I know because you have an icon. Are you literate? Can you write and do sums?"

"Yes, Highness."

"Then what is the problem?"

"I am only eighteen!"

"I am also eighteen, and I arrived in Constantinople at age seventeen, not knowing know how to be the consort of the co-emperor. I learned."

"Princess Anthusa said that the Emperor hasn't declared that the monastery will be reconsecrated as a convent." I held my breath. I was arguing with a princess!

She scowled. "Anthusa knows nothing. The Emperor promised me this convent. He does not break his promises."

"Highness, I beg you, pick someone else."

Her voice was low and intense. "I must have this convent and you must be abbess. I will tell you why. Then you will stop arguing. Are you listening?"

"Yes, Highness."

"If this child I carry is born malformed or God forbid, female, Leon will demand a divorce. Empress Evdokia will back him and the Emperor will bow to her will. He will exile me to that prison convent on Lesbos where everyone dies. I must escape. I will beg them to let me come here to pray. When I get here, a fisherman will take me to Kallipolis on the far side of the Propontis Sea. Merchant ships are always docked at Kallipolis; I saw them when we passed through the Dardanellia passage on the warship coming here from Athens. Some of the merchant ships are owned by Jews. They feel no loyalty to the Emperor. They will take me to Italy. The pope will give me sanctuary. He holds no love for the Emperor."

"Highness, I understand your need for this convent. An experienced abbess will serve you better. I will find one for you."

Her voice got sharp. "Every abbess will be a spy for the empress. You, I can trust. You owe me, Sister Thekla. I got you out of prison. I returned your icon to you."

And you will throw me in prison if I don't do what you want, I thought. We were nearly through the village. The harbour was just ahead. Princess Irini lowered her voice.

"Tell the stonemason to build an escape tunnel under the convent walls. He has to finish before the renovations start. No one can know but him. Go now and tell him. Now."

Irini of Athens looked straight at me with those piercing dark eyes. I took a deep breath. I owed her my life. She had brought me back Saint Thekla. I had stood beside the silk-sailed warship taking her to Constantinople and I had looked up at her and known that our fates would join. Now I knew why Saint Thekla had brought us together. I was the only person she could trust.

"Yes, Princess."

"Then get on the yacht. You are coming to the Great Palace with me. I will ask Emperor Constantine to appoint you as haristikaris and abbess."

I couldn't breathe. I had run away from Ikonion because my father was going to put me in a convent. And now I would be an abbess? What a turn life had taken! Then the words of the monk soothsayer in Filomelion came into my ears. "You will have a difficult and complicated life, that is clear," he had said. "You will rise as high as an empress, no, higher,"

His prediction of a difficult and complicated life had come true, yet I was still alive. As for the part about rising as high as an empress, here I was, keeping company with a princess who might one day become empress—if she survived. Now, I was on my way to the Great Palace! I touched my precious icon. Saint Thekla would have to guide me.

The Empress Irini Series

Book 1:
Betrothal &
Betrayal

In order of appearance. *Fictional characters are in italics.*

Thekla of Ikonion – *young woman from village near Ikonion in the centre of the Empire of the Romans of the East who walks for months to Constantinople in search of her betrothed.*

Saint Thekla of Ikonion First Woman Saint and Equal to the Apostles – young woman from Ikonion who was sainted for leaving her family to follow Saint Paul to Rome, in the process performing many miracles.

Myrizikos – *young man from village near Ikonion who is betrothed to Thekla.*

Father Damianos – *village priest in Thekla's village.*

Emperor Constantine V – Emperor of the Roman Empire of the East, powerful military commander and skilled administrator.

Co-emperor Leon IV – son of Emperor Constantine and his first wife, marries Irini of Athens at age 19.

Princes Christoforos, Nikiforos, Nikitas, Evdokimos, and Anthimos – sons of Emperor Constantine and his third wife Empress Evdokia.

Mihalis the Dragon – distinguished military commander.

Elias– *monk of mysterious background who travels with Thekla to Constantinople.*

Auntie Sofia – *wealthy woman of Nicaea, aunt of Elias.*

Empress Evdokia – third wife of Emperor Constantine V, mother of five of his sons and one daughter.

Irini of Athens – born in Athens, orphan raised in the house of her uncle, taken by Emperor Constantine by warship to Constantinople to marry his son, Co-emperor Leon.

Patriarch Constantine – Ecumenical Patriarch, head of the Eastern Orthodox Church.

Patriarch Nikitas the Slav – Ecumenical Patriarch, head of the Eastern Orthodox Church appointed by Emperor Constantine V to replace Patriarch Constantine.

Eleni – *prostitute in a brothel in Constantinople.*

Abbess Pulkeria – *abbess of Ta Gastria convent in Constantinople.*

Princess Anthusa – only daughter of Emperor Constantine and Empress Evdokia

Akepsimas – *cook in the household of Patrikia Constanta*

Patrikios Leon – wealthy accountant in the tax office in the Great Palace, father of Megalo.

Patrikia Constanta – *wife of Patrikios Leon.*

Aspasia – *assistant cook in the household of Patrikia Constanta.*

Megalo – daughter of Patrikios Leon, engaged to Fanis.

Doti – based on Theodote, widowed mother of Fanis,

attendant to Princess Irini.

Tisti – based on Theoktiste, mother of Theodore, attendant to Princess Irini.

Fanis – based on Theophanes, betrothed to Megalo.

Doctor Moses – based on physician from Antioch in the Caliphate.

Andreas – *medical assistant to Doctor Moses.*

Abbess Anthusa – Abbess of the convent at Mantinia who predicted the healthy birth of Empress Evdokia's twins Anthusa and Christoforos.

Abbess Fanouria – *Abbess in the Convent of Saint Emmelia in Bithynia.*

Father Dimitrios – *village priest on the island of Prinkpos near Constantinople.*

Theo – based on Theophylaktos, cousin of Irini of Athens who accompanied her to Constantinople.

Note: The IRINI OF ATHENS series covers the years 752 AD – 803 AD. During this time these people called themselves Romans of the East. They are now called the Byzantines.

Biographical data is available at http://www.pbe.kcl.ac.uk/data/index.html, Prosopography of the Byzantine Empire.

Glossary

Aegean Sea – body of water between mainland Greece and Turkey

Amorion – fortified Roman city in Anatolia and large military base

anagrapheus – tax official

Anassa, Amma – terms of respect for an abbess

Anatolia – Large theme in the centre of the Empire of the Romans, now central Turkey

Antioch – wealthy city in the Caliphate

artopios – bread vendor

Akimiti monks – monks who never sleep so they can continually pray

Augustaion – large area between the Church of Holy Wisdom and the Great Palace

biblioamphiastis – bookbinder

Bithynia – rich farming area near Constantinople

Blachernae Palace – Imperial Palace in Constantinople on the Golden Horn, said to have the Veil of the Virgin Mary

Bosporus Straits – narrow waterway connecting the Propontis Sea and the Pontus Sea (the Sea of Marmara and the Black Sea)

Caliphate – empire east of the Roman Empire of the East

Chalke Gate – entrance to the Great Palace in Constantinople, opposite the Church of Holy Wisdom

Cemetery of Pelagios – cemetery outside the walls of Constantinople where they throw the bodies of criminals

Chalkidon – (Chalcedon) city on the Propontis Sea opposite Constantinople

clamys – triangular cloak worn over one shoulder and fastened with a broach.

Church of the Virgin of the Copper Market – church in Constantinople that had the belt of the Virgin Mary.

Church of Holy Apostles – large church in Constantinople with the tombs of the emperors

Convent of the Mother of God on Prinkypos – convent on Prinkypos Island which Empress Irini of Athens had converted from a monastery and where she went on retreat

Kinammomon – the ancient Greek and Byzantine word for cinnamon

codex – book that came after scrolls (pl. codices)

Dalmatiou Prison – a prison in Constantinople

Daphne Palace – residence of the imperial family inside the Great Palace

Despina – title of respect for women

Diapompefsi – a public humiliation consisting of putting the victim naked backwards on a donkey and driven through the streets

Dorylaion – old Roman fortified city and military base

Ekloga – book of laws that governed the Empire of the Romans written by Emperor Leon the Isaurian

ekonomis – nun second in authority in a convent after the abbess

evkrata – a drink made from early sour apples

Evdomon – (Hebdomon) Military base seven miles

outside Constantinople

follis – a copper coin (pl. folles)

forum – a large square or oval space in a Roman city with statues, fountains, or important buildings; (pl. fora)

garum – fish sauce

gerokomia – old people's homes

Hall of Nineteen Couches – a vast reception hall inside the Great Palace

haristikaris – the manager of a convent

heteria – prostitutes (pl)

Hippodrome – arena in Constantinople for chariot racing

hiremporia – pork vendor

hypourgia – nurse, pl.

ikthyopratia – fish store

inopios – wine vendor

Kallipolis – (Gallipoli), town at the mouth of the Dardanelles, on the Sea of Marmara

kandilli – candelabra

kapelarion – a family restaurant

kapelarios – owner or waiter in a kapelarion

kathisma – the covered stand in the Hippodrome for the emperor and his family

kitron – similar to a lemon

koukla – little doll (term of affection)

kouritzaki – my little girl (term of affection)

krasopatera – wino monk (a curse)

kithara – stringed instrument, similar to a guitar

Lycus River – river that flows through Constantinople

lyre – like a hand-held harp

maforion – the head scarf of a nun (pl. maforia)

magerissa – nun in a convent who manages the kitchen and shops for provisions

magirio – bread bakery

makelarion – lamb and mutton vendor

Malagina – stud farm where horses were raised for the imperial army

malakismeni – a foul curse (wanker)

Magnavra Palace – Palace inside the Great Palace where the emperor receives visitors

Master Builder – a professional builder and architect at the top of his field

milaresion – a silver coin (pl. milaresia)

mizoteris – a paid housekeeper

Nakoleia – old Roman fortress and market town

Nicaea – walled city in Bithynia where the Ecumenical Councils were held

Nikomidia – busy market city in Bithynia

omorfia mou – my pretty girl (term of affection)

oxygala – a sour milk cheese similar to yogurt

pandoheus – innkeeper

pandohion – inn

pandokissa – innkeeper's wife

patrikios – high level position appointed by the emperor

paximadia – dried bread rusks that are softened with liquid

Pelagios Cemetery – Cemetery outside the walls of Constantinople where the bodies of executed criminals were thrown into an open pit

Pelekitis Monastery – monastery in Bithynia near

Constantinople

Pendykion – military fortress and town on the Propontis Sea

Piraeas – port city for Athens

plateia – an open area among the houses in a village where people gather

polykandillon – a hanging flat chandelier with glass holders for oil inserted into holes

pornovoskos – a man who buys girls from their fathers for prostitution

protarch – doctor who is chief of staff of a hospital

proyevma – breakfast

Propontis Sea – now called the Sea of Marmara

Prussa hot springs – hot mineral baths across the Propontis from Constantinople

Pontus Sea – now called the Black Sea

raptaina – seamstress

Saint's Eortologion – a yearly calendar listing the saints' days

Sampson Hospital – a large public hospital behind the Church of Holy Wisdom in Constantinople

Seflukia – port on the Roman Sea for Antioch

skaramangion – long, sleeveless garment worn over a tunica

skatopsychi – a foul curse

stratiotis – wife of a soldier

Studios Monastery – large monastery in Constantinople

Syke – port on the Roman Sea (Mediterranean) near the border to the Caliphate

szingi – fritters

Tagmata – Emperor Constantine's personal guard
theme – area of the empire similar to a province governed by a military commander
thymelikia – dancers
tonsure – the shaved part on a monk's head
trahana – a mixture of a grain and dried milk used to thicken soups and stews
valanissa – attendant in a public bathhouse
Veil of the Virgin – a scarf at Blachernae Palace said to have belonged to the Virgin Mary
verjuice – a drink made from unripe grapes
xenodohos – the admitting clerk in a hospital
zamnykistria – a sambucca player

Explore the Empress Irini Series

Book 1
Betrothal & Betrayal
Seventeen-year-old Thekla needs her quick wits and knife to track down her betrothed, a soldier who has left her at the altar for the third time. Elias the monk travels with her to Constantinople where she meets Irini of Athens, an extraordinarily beautiful orphan her same age who has been brought by powerful Emperor Constantine to marry his son, Co-emperor Leon. The two women join forces to survive this vigorous capital of the Roman Empire of the East which is rocked by religious and political strife. But will Thekla help the ambitious and ruthless Irini of Athens find the power that she craves?

Book 2
Poison is a Woman's Weapon
Irini's conniving mother-in-law, her five jealous step-brothers, and her own husband threaten Irini's safety in Constantinople. She summons Abbess Thekla, her knife-wielding friend, to bring her sharp wits and courage to get Irini safely through childbirth in the Great Palace. Thekla owes Irini her life and thus her loyalty but she is staggered by Irini's powerful ambitions which far exceed being docile wife and mother. Can Thekla survive Irini's vengeful nature and the bloody aftermath of Irini's ruthless ambition?

Book 3
Seizing Power
Constantine's father, Co-emperor Leon, dies unexpectedly, making Constantine emperor at age nine with Irini as Regent. Abbess Thekla's loyalty to Irini shifts to Constantine as she watches Irini block his authority and keep the power herself. Irini makes Constantine wed the disliked Maria, prevents the Senate from naming him Emperor in his own right at age 18, and imprisons him when he tries to stop her henchmen from amassing wealth and power. Constantine's army friends free him, arrest her, and raise him to the throne. Resourceful as ever, Irini will not be thwarted. Can Thekla prevent them from murdering each other?

Book 4
The Price of Eyes
In the final book, Irini returns to the throne. She tricks Constantine into divorcing Maria and exiles her and Constantine's two daughters to Abbess Thekla's island convent where Maria goes mad. Irini misleads Constantine into taking revenge on the soldiers who arrested her and the empire erupts into civil war, army against army, Irini against Constantine. Fearing for her life, Irini traps Constantine, wounding his eyes, but Thekla rescues him. Irini is finally empress in her own right. But will Thekla help her hold the throne?

Janet McGiffin lives in Manhattan and Washington State. She started her writing career writing obituaries for a small-town newspaper and went on to work for the Milwaukee Health Department and as a press officer for the Washington state Senate where she gained first-hand knowledge for her mystery series featuring Doctor Maxene St. Clair. While living in Greece, she wrote grant proposals for non-profit women's organizations, two English language easy readers for Cambridge University Press, hiking articles for greecetravel.com, and a humour column for the Athens News newspaper—all research for her Empress Irini Series.